A PUZZLE OF MURDER

A SEABREEZE BOOKSHOP COZY MYSTERY BOOK 4

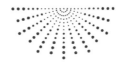

PENNY BROOKE

*A*lways on the move, Honey Lindstrom was a blur as she opened the oven and pulled out the crostini with apple and smoked gouda. Each one was topped, of course, with just a drizzle of honey, which was ever-present in her shop. She pirouetted gracefully to finish boxing up the trays of tiny cupcakes.

She had outdone herself on those, each one decorated with a little frosted book, a beach umbrella in bright colors, or a golden orb of sun. She could not only master flavors; Honey was an artist. The colors of the suns spread out in squiggly orange and reddish rays of icing.

"Almost done!" she said, dipping her head in a bashful smile. "Then once your party starts, Rue, summer can begin."

It was widely acknowledged here in Somerset Harbor that the official start to the busy summer season was the Summer Reading Celebration at the Seabreeze Bookshop. Like my gran before me, I scheduled the event about two weeks before the influx of tourists who flooded into Cape Cod and the surrounding towns like ours for the summer months. It was a way for the locals to have some final "just-us" time before the rush began.

The season would be ushered in that evening with beachballs and inflatable seahorses floating in kiddie pools beside the reading nooks and next to the registers. There would be local author signings and raffles for the books our staff had picked as best beach books of the year. (We got to read ahead of publication—a great perk of the job.)

Most of the decorations would stay up to greet the tourists, who we always hoped would arrive eager to fill their beach bags with new treasures from the Seabreeze Bookshop.

Books! To me and those who were my people, the right characters and plots could enhance a beach vacation just as much as the perfect rental property and the Catch of the Day at Alfredo's Kitchen. We sold a nice selection of sturdy canvas bags that would hold a lot of books. And we hoped, of course, our customers would fill those things right up.

The purchase of three books came with a bookish coozie. "Where Would You Like to Go Today?" was scrolled across the front. "Books Can Take You There!"

As for me, I read most of my beach books in September, when I had time to breathe. September was my time for sun and sand, and the beaches were still nice at that time of year. I was thankful for the tourists, who kept our business in the black, but by the time the first nip of coolness hit the air, I was thankful for the rest and the slower pace of life.

"Look for me there!" said Honey. "I need the perfect book to escape my life." The wry smile on her pretty face showed more amusement than a real need to escape, although I sensed that Honey had too much on her plate these days. In addition to being the town's go-to caterer, she had moved in with her Uncle Thomas, who was getting on in years and needed Honey's help. He was in his eighties and set in his ways. It had to be a strain.

"I need a nice romance, maybe something even racy." She lowered her voice to a whisper, even though it was just the two of us in the shop. Well, there was Althea, the co-owner of Spoonful of Honey, but Althea wouldn't judge.

An impish grin spread across my friend's face as she

closed a box of cupcakes. "In the culinary world, I may be the 'honey girl,' but I like my novels spicy."

"Well, I can fix you up for sure," I told her with a giggle. Recommending books to the romance readers of Somerset Harbor came with its own set of special challenges. I made it a point to be aware of any scenes that might send readers in to rail at me about indecency— and right here on the shelves of a respected store. In truth, those were the same scenes that brought some women in the next day looking for the sequel. And if you thought you could guess who was a fan or not, I'd bet you anything you would be surprised.

As Honey rang me up, I noticed dark circles underneath her eyes, a change that only grew apparent when she stood under the harsh light. I could just imagine what life was like at home. Things with her Uncle Thomas had steadily grown worse by the time those close to him decreed he could no longer live alone. The final straw had been when he almost sent the kitchen up in flames making crispy honey chicken. There was almost crispy *everything* on the property that day.

The Carroways could, of course, afford to hire the most elite of caregiver services for Thomas. It didn't have to be this way with Honey running herself ragged. Thomas Carroway had money to do…well, to do whatever suited the man's fancy at the moment; money was no object. Thomas was the latest family member to own and manage the distinguished family brand. Carroway Fine Honey had long been renowned by foodies. But Thomas had grown finicky in his later years. The family patriarch did not want strangers looking after him; Thomas wanted family. Unfortunately for Honey, the family had dwindled to just her and her sister.

She wrapped up a pineapple cheeseball, which had always been my favorite. "I'm taking a quiche home in a bit to warm up for Uncle Thomas," she told me as she worked. "Then I'll head over to the store."

"Hey, how is your uncle doing?" I paused to look her in the eye. "More importantly, Honey, how are *you*?"

She shrugged. "He's really sweet, so there is that. He has never been one of those cranky older men who get so demanding. The problem is his mind—which is kind of going. He really should retire, but for a workaholic like he is, taking away his briefcase is like taking away the newest, flashiest Xbox from a kid."

"Oh, my."

Honey leaned across the counter. "For example, last week, he mistook *the coatrack* for his accountant Archer Fancher."

We both burst into giggles, too polite to say that Archer Fancher was a bit more...rounded, shall we say?...than any coatrack that we knew of.

7

Honey paused to stare distractedly at a paper to her side, then she turned to me. "The coat hanging on the rack *did* look kind of like the raincoat Archer sometimes wears," she said with a shrug.

"You always see the bright side."

"And the good news is that Uncle Thomas was talking sense about accounts receivable and all that other business—which is sometimes not the case."

"Well, then I do hope the coatrack gave him sound advice." I checked my phone for the time.

"If not, he can always ask the upholstered accent chair. Bea is always going on and on about what a 'smart' piece it is."

Bea was Honey's sister, although I had never found the two to have a single thing in common besides their last name.

"At least the bills are getting paid." My friend rolled her eyes. "Or the checks are being *written* and put into envelopes. I found them yesterday—in a refrigerator drawer, stuck between a pack of bacon and a wedge of cheese."

"Are you telling me that Thomas still writes out checks himself?" That was craziness to me. (Well, that and the cold storage.) The company was successful enough that I assumed he had people for those things. Honey's aging uncle had for a long time worked from an office in the rambling family mansion with minimal staff there. But Carroway Fine Honey also owned a two-story brick historic building in the south of downtown with a staff of about twenty-five.

"He's...oh, Rue, I don't know—a little paranoid, I think. For the past few years, he's insisted on being more hands-on with anything to do with money. Until the memory slips—which are something new—that would have been fine, I guess. But he has always been a big-picture type of guy. A man of ideas rather than a detail, number person." She folded a flap on one of the bags of food and sealed it with a sticker featuring her trademark spoon design.

"Oh, don't get me wrong," she said. "A lot of the innovations and new programs over the last decades have come from Uncle Thomas. Even when his father was the one in charge and Thomas was VP." She set aside the bag. "Like the Bee Your Best Scholarships at Somerset Harbor High and the honeybun kiosks that we've set up all up and down the beach."

"He's beloved in the town," I said. "That much is for sure."

"Oh, no doubt about it," she said with a frown. "It's just that Thomas is the dreamer, and he needs other people to make the calls, to set up the schedules, and to do whatever. With that kind of stuff, he's helpless, and he always has been. He's always had assistants, but now they never last. Last month, he fired three."

✐"Honey, that's not good." I really had to go, but I could tell she needed somebody to vent to. "Who does he have left?"

"Just one secretary and one maid left at the house." She sighed. "He just seems to want to keep kind of to himself; says he likes a quiet house." She frowned. "It's because his mind is going, which is really sad to see. He was always brilliant in his way." Then her frown melted into a teasing smile. "But he can't fire me. I'm family." She laughed and rolled her eyes. "Lucky, lucky me."

"It sounds like you're a saint."

She winked. "Remind me, Rue, to tell you about my last date with *Paul*. I am *not* a saint—but we sinners sure have fun."

Paul Budd. He owned a chain of upscale smoothie restaurants around Somerset Harbor and Cape Cod. With intense green eyes, Mediterranean dark good looks, and muscles for days and days, Paul was quite the catch. And living with an uncle who needed round-the-clock assistance must really do a number on the love life of a sweet young thing like Honey, I decided. Staff was there in the day, but Honey could only leave at night for a little while.

"You are a saint," I repeated.

"But he's family, and he thanks me, Rue, a million times a day. Plus, I kind of feel I owe him. When Bea and I were little, he was the fun adult who'd set up water slides at the mansion; he'd teach us magic tricks. It was like one big playground over at his place. He would make up these characters—animals who lived in the kitchen cupboards and who'd come out to play when Bea and I would visit. You should have heard the voices he would use, Rue. Like the chicken who had hiccups—that one was my favorite." She let out a sigh. "Now it's my turn to help him. Because we're family, right?"

The Foo Fighters played quietly in the background as she carefully placed a box of spinach balls into a second bag of food. In the back, I caught a glimpse of Althea, who was singing to the music as she frosted what looked to be a carrot cake. With Althea's bright pink hair and the streak of green running through Honey's blonde, the kitchen had a kind of unicorn/rainbow feel.

Honey glanced again, distracted, at the paper on the counter. I moved close enough to see it was a drawing of a line of trees—some tall, some round, and some with spreading branches. All of them seemed to be laughing heartily at something, like this was *the* party in the forest no tree would want to miss.

"Interesting," I said.

"Well, that's one word you could use," she said with a frown. "Oh, just never mind. I have put a little something extra in the bags for you today." Her face lit up at the thought. "Bacon-wrapped Brussels sprouts! Let me know the verdict of your summer-reading crowd, and if it is a yes, we might just have a brand-new menu item here at Spoonful of Honey."

"My idea!" Althea called from the back of the small shop. She was carefully drawing or writing something on the cake. "I just had a craving. For bacon, Brussels sprouts, and a bit of balsamic. And then I thought, *Aha!*"

Honey nodded with approval. "When Althea's hungry, great ideas are born."

"That sounds amazing," I said. "I can't wait to try one of everything." I grabbed a bag along with a large cake box. "Well, I guess I should be going. I should be okay on time, but there are always anxious readers who like to show up early."

"I say let them in and put them all to work!" suggested Honey. "They can arrange the cupcakes in pretty patterns on your table. And, hey, if they are avid readers, use them for promotion! Plant some ideas in their heads about the books you'd like to sell, and let them spread the word."

Honey, with her spiky pixie cut and her Dr. Who T-shirt, hardly looked the type to be savvy about sales and strategies to build a business. But Honey knew her stuff. The Carroway business acumen was firmly in place for the next generation, running strongly through the veins of this baking, menu-planning wunderkind. Spoonful of Honey was only tangentially related to the bigger family business, but she and Bea would supposedly inherit and carry on the family honey brand one day.

She grabbed a stack of boxes and walked me to my car.

"See you in a bit," I said once things were loaded in the trunk. "I have some books in mind I think you'll really like. We just got in a new romance set in the Scottish Highlands. It's kind of a retelling of 'The Princess and the Pea'—with a murder thrown in too."

Honey's eyes grew wide.

Hooked her, Rue. Good job.

"Know your customer, my dear," my gran had advised me when I took over the shop for her. And there were three things I understood about my favorite caterer: She had a trip to Scotland booked for spring (with a nurse in place to watch over Thomas). Honey was a faithful member of our True Crime Book Club. And she spent as much time in the children's section as she did browsing the romances.

"Sometimes when life is hard, you just have to close your eyes and imagine you're a princess," she had once explained, and that made sense to me. One would be surprised how many children's books are bought by grown-ups for themselves. And why not? The timeless wisdom you first learned at six still holds true at sixty. Winnie-the-Pooh was still one of the wisest souls I knew, and he had a place of honor on the bookshelves of my store.

But enough about all that; tonight was party night.

"Thanks for the great food," I said. "It will be delicious. See you in a bit."

She held up a hand. "Wouldn't miss it, Rue. And Uncle Thomas goes to bed so early I can surely get away for an hour or so." She laughed and shook her head. "Unless the coatrack orders me to stay in—or the china cabinet is insistent that I must stay put." She lifted an eyebrow. "I swear to you that lately, my whole life has been just nuts. So if Honey Lindstrom doesn't show up at your soirée, you should for sure send in the troops."

Something in her eyes made me anxious for her. My friend Elizabeth liked to tease that since I'd never had a daughter, I worried obsessively about the younger women who frequented my store.

True to form, I studied Honey for a moment. "You sure that you're okay?"

"Oh, yeah. You know, families and business. It's always something, right?"

I did understand. My gran was so supportive, but sometimes when I ran a new idea by her on the phone, just the slightest pause on the other end could make me doubt myself.

A light rain began to fall as I got in and started up my car. Cozy reading weather (excellent for business), but I did hope the clouds would hold off till my customers were home and their stomachs full. And, of course, with their beach bags—twenty percent off tonight—all stuffed with captivating reads.

CHAPTER TWO

wo hours later, the celebration was in full force, and the store was full to bursting. A line snaked through the cooking section, where Cami Bentley from The Seafood Shack was signing her new book, *Not Your Grandma's Appetizers*. It likely didn't hurt that she'd set out sample plates of melon-prosciutto skewers along with crab dip on slices of baguette.

My friend Andy hovered near me as I straightened up some books. *"Not Your Grandma's Appetizers?"* He raised an eyebrow at me. *"My* grandma, I'll have you know, made a perfect crab dip. Didn't everyone's?"

"Oh, hush with you," I told him. "I'm sure that there's some exciting twist for modern types like us."

He smiled, a twinkle in his eyes. With a small paunch around the middle and wrinkles underneath his eyes, he was my oldest friend in town; he had promised my gran he would do his best to look after me.

Of course, I was a grown woman, thank you very much, with no need for anybody to look after me. But I could always use a friend, and Andy was a dear one. He could, of course, get a little cranky when I asked too many questions. But what a shame to have a friend who was a private eye and not get a little gossip out of the situation. Besides, Andy understood I was good at keeping secrets.

Now, I gave him a wink. "Make yourself useful, Andy, and take some food to Elizabeth if you would be so kind."

Elizabeth, my business partner, looked busy at the welcome table, encouraging our guests to choose a sticker that described them best: "Books make me miss my bedtime," for example. Or "I talk back to characters I meet in my books." When it was their time to check out, they would learn which prize was associated with the sticker they had chosen. Free bookmark, twenty percent off, and so on. Surprises for everyone tonight!

Jana, who helped us part-time, had queued a summer-book-themed playlist. She was swaying to the Beatles' "Paperback Writer" now as she rang up a customer. "Enjoy your books," I heard her say.

I was heading to the front to greet the mayor when I

felt a cold nose against my knee, and I heard a happy yip. My golden retriever, Gatsby, was in his element tonight. The big sweet, friendly dog loved nothing more than a customer, and many of our regulars would come in with treats tucked inside their pockets. Tonight, almost all of Gatsby's favorite people had appeared at once, along with brand-new friends. Like the perfect host, my gentle dog had gone from one person to another, making all feel welcome. Every now and then, he'd pause to turn in gleeful circles.

On the other hand, the rest of our pet trio were a little wary of the mass of people who'd come in to crowd the aisles of books—which, in the minds of the bookstore cats, *belonged* to the cats. Oliver, the smallest, had scrunched himself into a ball of snow-white fur. He peered out at the scene from behind a thick volume on world history. Occasionally, a high-pitched "Aww!" could be heard coming from that section, and Oliver would purr and accept a little petting.

Beasley was even more bashful than his brother— except for a select few customers who had won his heart. That night, he was a fast gray blur, who would occasionally scurry over to press against my ankles.

Now, I felt him move against my feet, tickling my skin, and I bent to pick him up. "Happy Summer

Reading Celebration," I whispered in his ear. "Get used to the crowds, Bease. Busy season's coming!"

I was both excited and a little tired already.

The cat nestled his head into my chest, then his head shot up and his eyes grew wide as the bell jingled on the door. It had been a frequent sound that night, yet Beasley still looked startled. It was what made him precious—the way he was constantly amazed at the ordinary and routine. He scurried beneath my desk to hide from the newcomer.

I looked up toward the door. *Well, of course,* I thought. *I get you, my sweet kitty.* I was not so glad to see this particular visitor any more than my wary cat was. It was Honey's sister, Bea. With her dark hair piled elegantly atop her head, she looked around the store. Her expression was full of purpose—and superiority.

I did not believe I had ever sold a single book to Bea; Bea was not a reader. She had come here not to buy but to be seen and to schmooze with potential customers for her business, Exquisite Beach Designs. Bea loved nothing more than to play with pricey furniture and fabrics and zillion-dollar "statement pieces" for the mantle. Like her sister, Bea had the Carroway drive for success running through her veins. But with Bea, there was no joy in the human interaction. There was just a single-minded quest for dollars to fund the kinds of things she thought set her apart. Like the floral-print wrap dress and red Jimmy Choos, so impractical for tonight, with the rain now falling hard.

I caught Elizabeth's eye, and we exchanged a covert look. There were times, of course, Dolce & Gabbana could lend a woman elegance and flair. Here, it just made Bea look like she had shown up for a beach day dressed for a coronation.

Poor Elizabeth had been getting an extra dose this month of the imperious Bea Lindstrom. Elizabeth had decided to redo the downstairs of her house, and Bea was her chosen designer—just because we both loved Honey.

Where was Honey anyway?

Reg Adams, who ran the men's clothing store next door, clapped a friend on the back. He was talking up the upcoming fundraiser, I could tell, for the local food bank. Reg served on the board, and people always knew when they shopped for a suit with Reg, they should bring a can of beans or soup to leave in the box at the door.

Now, he was reaching out to shake the hand of another man—just as Bea was, unfortunately, passing with her wine. She gave a little yelp and stopped short, but there was no harm done. A little bit of wine landed on the floor, but the designer dress and the Jimmy Choos remained immaculate.

"Oh! I am *so sorry*, Bea." Reg gave her an apologetic smile, holding his hand to his heart. "I do hope you're okay."

Her response—so Bea-like—was to glare. "Is it really that hard, Reg, to be aware of your surroundings?" Red-faced, she moved on.

Harry Potter on a Broom! Bea was even more obnoxious than she was on a normal night—and at my party too. I watched her throughout the evening. In a sea of happy people, she was the discordant note, a scowl always on her face. She scowled at the pirate ship bobbing in the kiddie pool. She scowled at the cheese-stuffed mushrooms her sister had prepared. Jana had set the platter out beside a figurine of Alice and her magic mushroom.

At one point, I dared to approach her, asking if she had heard from Honey. "She told me she was coming, and I put some books aside," I said.

For the thousandth time, Bea scowled. "Who even knows with Honey? Probably catering to the every whim of our foolish Uncle Thomas."

I'd always wished I had a sister. At other times I was so very thankful to be an only child.

When Reg passed me a little later with a stack of

Michael Connelly paperbacks, I gave him a sympathetic smile. "I am so sorry, Reg. Bea's behavior back there was unforgivable, and I apologize that it happened in my store."

He threw his head back and laughed. "Well, my wife is always saying that I'm trouble when I get too close to something that could spill or break. But, Rue, it's really fine." He gave me a wink. "There was enough left in her glass to hopefully help the woman chill," he told me quietly. "And she's not half bad, you know. She talks a tough game, Bea does, but"—he lowered his voice even more—"when we ran short last Christmas at the food bank, do you know who swooped in with a huge—and highly confidential—gift that put us over the top?"

"No, Reg. You don't mean it." Like her sister, Bea would someday have all the money in the world to give away—but at the present time, she was far from rich.

"As I say, Bea is not without her good side," Reg continued. "One just never knows."

"Hmm." I paused to take that in. "Remind me not to judge," I said. (Or to give Reg any info that was "highly confidential.")

My mind was soon swept up in the business of selling and recommending books. I caught up on a lot of news about the prep work going on for the busy season. Then, as the night came to a close, I began the cleanup, stuffing paper goods and trash into bags. The leftovers I divided up between myself, Elizabeth, Jana, and Andy, who had stayed to help.

Elizabeth seemed winded as she stooped to gather a discarded napkin. Her long gray hair today was swept to the side with a rhinestone comb, and she wore a long, multicolored skirt and white cotton peasant top.

As we were locking up, I turned to Andy, something weighing on my mind. "You know, Honey never showed, and she swore she would."

"Things happen." Andy shrugged.

I reached into my purse and sent her a quick text. "Missed you tonight! Everything still good?"

When I got no response, I thought about what she had told me earlier: *I swear to you that lately, my whole life has been just nuts. So if Honey Lindstrom doesn't show up at your soirée, you should for sure send in the troops.*

There had been a look in Honey's eyes I'd never seen before. Until now, I'd brushed her comment off as a little Honey humor. But something just felt off.

"Andy, we should check on Honey."

"Rue," he said with the exaggerated patience he reserved for only me. "There's a reason I am the detective and you deal in fiction."

And biography and true crime and real-world commentary, but that was neither here nor there.

"In the world outside your novels," he continued, "it is no cause for alarm for someone to be tired and decide to skip a party."

"Oh, I know you're right, but there's a certain thing as instinct. And I have it, and you don't." Alarm bells were going off even louder now, but hopefully, a quick trip to the mansion on the hill would soon quell my fears.

My friend let out a sigh. "Well, you and Gatsby go ahead and pile into my car, and I'll drive you over there." He had learned when I was insistent, he might as well just humor me and get it over with.

But the "quick trip" to the mansion did not quell my fears; it set my heart to racing as Gatsby barked, alarmed, at the sea of blue police lights.

"What the..." Andy screeched to a stop. "Rue, you stay right here, and I'll go see what's up." He gave me that Andy look that meant, "Don't even try to argue."

He hurried through the massive wrought iron gates and up the winding steps to the sprawling white stone house that looked somewhat castle-like. It looked rather ominous as well as it stretched toward the sky with its turreted, multilevel roof.

To try to still my heart, I climbed into the back of Andy's blue Sonata and pressed myself against my dog—who whined sympathetically to me.

Hurry, Andy, hurry.

But when he returned, his face was grim. I hated it sometimes when my instincts were correct.

He got in beside me and reached for my hand. "Rue…" He paused and squeezed his eyes shut, and I knew it was bad.

"Rue," he said in an almost whisper, "your dear friend is gone."

CHAPTER THREE

"*W*hat?"

A chill ran up my spine.

"I don't understand. Like, not-breathing gone? Or are you telling me that Honey up and disappeared?" *Please let it be that.*

But his eyes and his silence told me it was the former.

Tears pricked at my eyes. "How can she be *gone?*"

Andy took a breath. "Thomas Carroway made the call about an hour ago, it seems. Apparently, Honey fell asleep in the TV room this evening after work, and she just…passed away, as far as they can tell."

"But, Andy, that's insane. She was in her twenties! She was fine! Three hours ago, I swear, she was doing all her food-prep stuff, packing up my order. How could she just die?" *Had someone murdered Honey?*

"Thomas said she seemed...well, she hasn't seemed herself in the past few weeks. Apparently, she came home and sat down to read—but right away she fell asleep," Andy reported with a frown. "Thomas tried to wake her since it was getting time for dinner, but there was no response, no movement. He felt she was *too still,* and he sensed then that she was gone." Andy shook his head. "The old man is a mess."

"Yeah, it sounded like the two of them were close. From what I understood, he was pretty helpless without Honey here to help," I said. And who would help him now? Now there was just Bea, and, well, good luck with that.

"They'll do toxicology, of course, to check for signs of foul play—because she was so young," reported Andy in a somber voice. "But there were no signs of trauma. No reason for the cops to think this might have been anything other than a natural—but unexpected—death." Andy could get the scoop because he was one of them. Not officially—at least not anymore, since he'd opened up his private investigative office. But they often called on him when they needed extra hands—or when they were stumped. Andy was the best.

"You know, I have a feeling, Andy, there is something fishy here."

He gave me a look. "Rue, what has occurred is tragic, but whatever might have gone on in that house, the cops, I assure you, will get to the bottom of it."

"Who was there when Honey died?"

"It was just her and her uncle as far as we can tell. But who really knows? The old guy's memory isn't what it was, they say. His mind is pretty jumbled." Andy paused. "But Rue, there really is no need to—"

"Let's run inside for just a minute. I just have a feeling Thomas needs me, Andy." My hand was, in fact, already on the handle of the door.

"As I say, there is no need for you to get involved. Listen to me, Rue. They've called Bea to stay the night."

"Bea has no idea that Thomas will only take his medicine if Honey sings to him. And that the parrot only eats cooked quinoa and bananas." We had to take good care of that bird, who was like a child to Thomas; Thomas had already lost too much. There was no way in the world that Bea would sing to the old man while he took his pills. And there was certainly no way she would get a pan out and cook quinoa for a parrot.

I could not do much for Honey, but I could do this. "I'm going in," I said. I grabbed Gatsby's leash and hurried toward the house.

Andy trotted along behind me, breathing hard to keep up with my quick steps. "Hold up for a minute. This is a possible crime scene! You really shouldn't, Rue."

A young cop glanced at me, alarmed, as I swung the big door open and strolled through the high-ceilinged foyer with its polished hardwood floors. Huge oil paintings were hung on the walls, framed in ornate gold.

"We're with him," I said as I turned to nod at Andy, who still struggled to keep up.

Gatsby gave an urgent bark as if to back me up.

Defeated and out of breath, Andy gave the cop a wave to indicate it was okay to let me and Gatsby in.

I made my way into the den and looked cautiously around the room. When Andy caught up with me, I asked, "Honey! Is she still…"

Andy shook his head. "The medical examiner's office has already left with Honey." He put a hand on my arm. "Rue, she isn't here."

I suppressed a sob. This was getting much too real, but I had work to do. I concentrated on the tasks I could do to help.

First, I made my way to Honey's uncle, who was bent over, breathing hard, on a green velvet high-backed couch. Tall and lanky, Thomas Carroway was all arms and legs and wrinkles with a bristly mustache. Carefully,

I lowered myself into the seat beside him, which was not an easy task. The couch, it seemed, had so many cushions there was barely room for people. It must have been picked by Bea.

"Thomas," I asked gently, "do you remember me? I am a friend of Honey's." I'd been by the house a few times to grab Honey for a movie or to go out on Thursday nights for all-you-can-eat crab legs at the Mermaid's Grotto. Each time, the secretary said she'd be happy to stay late to keep an eye on Thomas while Honey had some fun.

Now he looked at me with rheumy eyes, as if he were in a daze. "You say you knew my niece?"

"I did, and if they are through with you for a moment, I believe you have some medicine to take." I looked to a female officer nearby, who nodded that it was okay for me to steal his attention for a moment. Then perhaps I could put the man to bed if they were through with him. And had he even eaten?

His eyes moved to Gatsby, who gave a sympathetic growl.

"Is that a *golden wolf?*" asked Thomas, his eyes growing wide. "How extraordinary. And how well behaved."

Yes, he was losing it, and the stress likely didn't help.

"Be right back," I said.

"Be right back! Right back!" echoed a loud and raspy voice.

I turned, startled, to my left. I'd forgotten all about the parrot, whose name, I believed, was Zeke. The huge bird cocked his head at me and stared.

I put my hand to my chest and breathed. Then I headed out to look for some heart pills, which Honey had once mentioned she gave her uncle after dinner. Since Honey hadn't woken up to give her uncle any dinner, that would seem to mean he hadn't taken those heart pills.

The den was open to the kitchen, and I headed that way, with Gatsby close behind. It was all gorgeous cherry wood and sleek stainless steel. The first drawer that I opened contained—*voila*—a jumble of pill bottles. I glanced at a few; they were all prescribed to Thomas, but I hesitated. How could I be sure he *hadn't* had his daily dose? What was I to do? Skip a pill or take a double dose; either one could have consequences.

That's when Bea strode in, a hard look in her eyes. *Oh, thank goodness.* I took a nice deep breath. At least some family was here to sort out the pills; that was not my place.

"What the heck is going on?" she demanded, looking from one officer to the other. There were three of them scattered throughout the kitchen and the den, making notes and taking photographs.

Then she wheeled around and focused her glare on me. *"Rue?* What in the world? What on Earth are *you* doing in my uncle's house?"

"I came to help." *And you're welcome.* I kept my tone cordial, knowing her sister had just died. "I knew it was important Thomas take his pills, and, well...perhaps he hasn't eaten."

She sighed. "Oh, Rue, you must forgive me. I've had such a shock. Is it really true my sister..."

"I'm afraid it is." I gently led her to an overstuffed gold chair with green silken pillows. Gatsby settled at her feet, as if he could be of comfort.

"An officer came by the house," she said, "and a neighbor brought me here. I was in no shape to drive." She glanced at a tall woman, who appeared to be in her sixties. "Thank you, Stella. You can go," said Bea. "Much appreciated!"

Stella nodded quietly before she eased out the door.

"This is just unreal," said Bea. New lines in her face made it appear she had aged ten years since I'd seen her at the bookstore. A few tendrils had come undone from her updo, and her red lipstick was a little smudged— which was so unlike Bea. "I just can't believe it, Rue." She closed her eyes and breathed. "Rue, what do you know?"

I explained how I'd come to check on Honey when she had not shown up, and I gave Bea the bits of detail (hardly any details, really) I had learned from Andy.

Bea gazed quietly at a stack of board games piled up in a corner. "She was always telling me I should come over to the house more often. She was always pushing for the three of us to have some game nights, the three remaining Carroways." (By name, the sisters officially were Lindstroms, but they had Carroway blood as well through their mother's line.)

"Honey had the idea it would be good for our uncle's mind for him to stack Jenga blocks and to guess whether it was Professor Plum in the study with a wrench or whatever," Bea continued.

Dante's Inferno here on Earth! A chill ran up my spine. And to think that here we were in a real-life game of Clue.

"She said it was for Uncle Thomas." Bea continued to stare forlornly at the stack of games. "But Honey loved to play. How she used to laugh and laugh, even when she lost. Win or lose, she didn't care. She just wanted to have fun." She let out a sigh. "Not that I ever sat down at the table and played a game with her. I am sad to say I had not done that in years. But she'd get some of the staff to play with her and Thomas sometimes after work, and she'd bring them all some snacks from Forkful of Honey."

"Spoonful," I corrected.

"Spoonful!" called the parrot.

"See? That's how much attention this big sister paid to her little sister's life."

"Well, we all get busy don't we?" I leaned closer to her. "That's just how families are. We don't expect...well, this." I shuddered at the *this*.

"No excuse," said Bea. "I worried some for Thomas, how frail he'd become. But I didn't give a second thought to Honey, who has always been her own self, so very self-sufficient. Scattered and impulsive, but she could always find a way to make things work out in her life—or at least that's what I thought." She paused. "Was she in trouble, Rue? She could have come to me. *Who did this to Honey?*"

It seemed Bea was thinking murder just like me.

"I'm sure they'll figure that all out," I said to her gently. But they could not bring Honey back; they could not make this okay.

An older female officer approached. "Ms. Lindstrom," she announced, "we have some questions for you if you would come with me."

"Thank you, Rue, for being here." Standing up, Bea gave me a little nod.

In the silence following her departure, I could hear Thomas being interviewed as well. "She seemed absolutely fine," he said. I could see him trembling in a seat around the corner, underneath a painting of him and his dad. The Thomas in the painting looked jubilant, confident, in charge, but those days were gone. Someone had thought, at least, to throw a blanket around his frail shoulders.

"She said she had a headache," he told the officer, "which is why she took a little lie-down. But she was planning to go out after dinner to a party. So how bad could she have felt?" His voice quavered at the end of every sentence. His voice was almost pleading. "How could she be gone?"

Exactly! was my thought. How could she be gone?

Suddenly, the respectful quiet in the room was broken by the parrot. "Girl, you watch that mouth of yours! Besmirch the family name!"

The room went silent as everybody paused to take that in.

With my heart beating hard, I looked around the room to see what might look out of place. Oh, I knew professionals were there to sort out all of that, but I have found professionals can overlook a certain type of clue. They look for *dramatic clues* about what might have gone down at the scene of a crime: bullet casings, broken windows, shattered lamps, and such. Often, though, it pays to look for the *quiet* signs of why someone might have chosen to snuff out a life. I'd spent many evenings staying up too late, turning *one more page*, anxious to piece together clues alongside the fictional detectives that I loved.

But my experience, sadly, was not limited to books. For an upscale town in a much-desired zip code so close to Cape Cod, we'd had a surprising number of murders here in Somerset. I may have gotten a bit too involved in solving some of them—for Andy's tastes at least. But some of the victims had been people who were close to me, and the contributions I had made had led to the cases being solved. Which was good for the victims' families, good for the town's reputation in the tourism industry, good for everybody. Most of all, good for justice. Andy absolutely had no reason to complain.

I sat back and took a good look around the room, which was, for the most part, pristine. Sally Densley had cleaned the mansion for twenty years almost and did a thorough job. I took note of just two signs of disorder. An empty mug—used by Honey, maybe Thomas?—sat on a table by the couch. And next to a closet, a box was full to overflowing with some jars of something amber-colored. About twelve of the jars were scattered on the floor around the box. *Highly unusual*, I thought. Honey had once told me that her Uncle Thomas was a stickler for an ordered home, especially since it doubled as a place of business.

I nonchalantly stood and made my way past the box as if I were searching for Andy or maybe even Bea. Gatsby followed quietly, sniffing at the jars.

Looking down at them, I quickly read the yellow label. "Honey Ginger Sauce. Liquid Gold!" it said.

Then I noticed that the closet door had been left ajar, just enough to see inside—where the whole space was filled, top to bottom, with boxes of the honey-ginger jars. There were so many boxes and loose jars, in fact, the door could not be closed.

"A lot of nerve!" the parrot screeched. "Don't you dare! Don't you dare!"

Again, everybody turned their heads.

Then Andy was beside me. "If we could interview a parrot," he said to me quietly, "we could wrap this thing right up."

Dr. Dolittle, where are you?

CHAPTER FOUR

$\mathcal{T}$he scene at work the next day was a total change from the festive party atmosphere we had just enjoyed. The sense of fun had gone the way of the withering balloons, whose reds and greens and yellows seemed to be in mourning now, fading in the burst of sun streaming through the windows.

"It makes no sense," said Elizabeth. With her hair pulled back tightly in an easy ponytail, she took a sip of tea as she unpacked some boxes to reclaim her corner of the store. While the event was going on, her tables had been temporarily transformed into the sweet-treats corner and a sign-up station for our summer reading clubs. Now, the area was morphing back to her usual display of vintage letters, postcards, photos, and the like.

Antiquities by Elizabeth had steadily grown in reputation through the years, enough so that collectors were inclined to make lengthy drives to peruse her carefully curated peeks into the past. It was the locals, though, who loved it most of all. New things were always coming in from dealers and estate sales in the local area. And one never knew when Grandpa might show up in a photo or have his signature on a card in a display of correspondence from the past.

We sold all kinds of stories at the Seabreeze Bookshop.

The whole town, however, was consumed today by a real-life tale—that broke everybody's hearts.

"And, if you can believe it, the whole time there was a witness!" I gathered a handful of the books partygoers had left out, and I returned them to their places.

"There was a witness, Rue?" Elizabeth's eyes were wide.

"Don't get excited yet. It was the uncle's parrot, Zeke. But he had a lot to say." I told her about the cryptic hints the parrot had screamed out. Then I paused to think about it. "*Someone* was mad at *someone* who argued in that room," I said. "Something to do with family honor? Or the family reputation. Something along those lines." I pondered that some more as I returned some cookbooks to their proper shelf.

Of course, the parrot could have been repeating talk

unrelated to the murder. An argument, for instance, between Honey and her uncle. From what I understood, he hated interference when it came to his work. But someone had to step in, and it turned out to be poor Honey who stepped into the fray.

Or could it have been that Honey was the one who confronted *him?* Had she discovered something bad as she delved into the business and lived within his rooms? Something not in keeping with the promise Carroway Fine Honey made to those it served? *Quality, Integrity, and Exquisite Taste.*

"Who was there in the house when Honey...passed away?" asked Elizabeth, her eyes filled with concern.

"Just her and Thomas that we know of. But there was only him to ask, and his memory is off. Honey talked to me about it when I picked up the food."

"Well, the family's kept *that* quiet. But who's to blame them, really? No one's business but their own." Elizabeth began to artfully arrange some vintage photographs of families on the beach around the local area. Above her, she had strung old postcards, mostly from Somerset Harbor and the other towns around Cape Cod. Some had the pictures facing out, and some displayed cursive greetings scrawled to friends back home fifty years ago or more. All of the cards showed beach themes—a display to welcome summer.

Elizabeth let out a sigh. "What will tell the story of our time, you think? A string of boring texts someone discovers on our phones? Where is the romance in that?"

"Written by a generation whose lives are so dang frazzled they can't be bothered to fully spell out words," I said with a laugh. "*Tonight,* for heaven's sakes, spelled with the number two? If I ever get too busy to type out *T* and *O,* please just shoot me now."

As we continued with our work, my thoughts circled back to the mystery at the mansion.

Elizabeth grabbed a stack of photos and began to organize. Her mind seemed to be in the same place my mind was. "I will say our friend Bea showed up to the party with an extra twist of nasty to go with her fine couture," said Elizabeth. "As if something had just happened to foul up her mood." She paused to look at me. "You don't suppose that Bea could have stopped by the mansion first and had it out with Honey about... well, who really knows?"

Don't you dare, the parrot had said.

Besmirch the family name.

A chill ran up my spine as I thought about her words. There were, after all, a lot of ways to kill someone without mussing up your lipstick—smothering them, perhaps, with a fancy pillow? And there *was* that empty mug in the room where Honey died.

But, oh, what was I thinking? Being uppity and rude was a far lesser crime than killing one's own sister!

"We shouldn't even go there," I said to Elizabeth. "I think you and I have read too many murder mysteries— with unrealistic and ultra-dramatic twists." I picked up a dirty napkin that we'd missed when cleaning up the trash.

As I moved around the store, straightening displays, I wondered who Andy and the others might be inter- viewing now. Maybe someone else had been at the house with Thomas when Honey came back home. If so, that would be good. That person might know some- thing: if somebody had upset my friend after I left her shop—or if she had changed her plans for the evening and invited someone over, someone who meant to do her harm.

"We should check out the staff," I announced, mainly to myself.

"We?" asked Elizabeth.

I shrugged. The cops, I knew, would do the basics, but I could be an extra eye; I could do that for Honey. I had a big advantage, I decided, over someone with a badge—because of the simple facts of how human nature worked. A lot of people tended to get nervous when approached by the police, even the most diligent, law-abiding types. But with a local merchant and a dear friend of Honey? With chatty, worried me, a person who knows something might spill a lot of things.

Perhaps it would be a good idea if I ran on over and checked in with Althea. In addition to possibly yielding clues, it would also be the kind and thoughtful thing to do. The girl must be reeling. Plus, things here at the bookshop were likely to be slow. Most of the town's readers had been in the night before and would be at home turning pages, devouring new worlds.

Or they'd be texting frantically, trying to learn more about the shocking news that, for most of them, had broken overnight. We were small enough in Somerset that most everybody knew everybody else. Most people had at least sampled Honey's famous cheese straws or been to a party where they ate too much of her honey sriracha chicken wings. Here in Somerset, we were all connected by a taste, a shared memory, a friend.

"Mind if I head out?" I reached for my purse.

"Oh, sure. Go on ahead," said Elizabeth. "I just bought some boxes from Heirloom Estates I'm anxious to dig into. Plus, that pomegranate tea I love finally came in. So I will be right here. I'll be sipping, I'll be sorting, and taking in the quiet."

The quiet normally felt good after a big soirée, but

today it just felt empty. All three pets were fast asleep in their separate corners as if *they* had been the ones who had put in all the work and were now due for long naps. Gatsby let out a loud snore. Well, I suppose that big fellow *had* worn his sweet self out making all the guests feel loved.

I looked around the store, my hands feeling empty. *Something.* I should take something to Althea. Then I dashed back to Self Help and grabbed a copy of *Just Breathe: Fifty Thoughts to Get You Through.* It was my go-to rec for customers who were going through a loss or just feeling overwhelmed. That was most of us these days, even at the beach, where the frantic pace of life was supposed to be turned down a notch.

"Don't forget," I called, "I stashed some mushrooms and crostini in the fridge, and there are cupcakes too." I never thought a cupcake, all pink and white and sprin-kled, could make me want to sob. Honey had frosted and decorated all the little cakes with such joy and care despite all the stressors that were on her mind.

I channeled all of my feelings into a determination to find out who and why, and I had a mission as I headed out the door.

CHAPTER FIVE

*a*s I got out of my car at Spoonful of Honey, I heard angry voices coming from inside.

"And I don't want to hear about you running your big mouth!" Althea sounded adamant. "I fixed it. It is *fixed!*" she said. Then her voice turned menacing, very unlike her. "And it better not get back to me that you were spreading gossip. After everything that's happened? Well, that would be just foul."

Speaking of foul (or fowl), her words kind of echoed what I'd heard from Zeke. *Watch that mouth of yours... Don't you dare.*

I had moved a little closer, not to miss a word, when a gray-haired bearded gentleman burst through the door. When he almost ran smack-dab into me, he stopped. The furor in his eyes dissipated just a little, and he held up a hand, as if in apology. "So sorry. You okay?" he asked.

"No harm done. Just startled." I put my hand to my chest. "And you? Are you all right?"

He shook his head, distracted, and turned away from me. He got into his car and slammed the door with a force. Then he screeched out of there in a white Volvo SUV—but not before I got the first three letters of his tag. As I said, "extra eyes." The Barnstable County tag showed he was local, but I didn't recognize him. Which likely meant he didn't read and didn't work downtown.

My curiosity aroused, I headed into the small brick shop. Althea was seated dejectedly at the counter, her head in her hands.

"Althea! How are you?" I let out a sigh. "I could not believe the news. Oh, hon, it's just so *wrong*."

She looked up at me, dazed. "I keep thinking she will breeze in—with one of her Honey stories about why she's running late, which were just hysterical. So I never could get mad." She blinked away a tear, then she shook her head. "I turned on some Bon Jovi earlier today; I just needed to move, and I couldn't take the silence. And would you believe that goofy me came up here in the front to *bump hips with Honey to the music,* like we always did? We always liked to dance when we cooked and cleaned." Her voice began to break, and she blinked away a tear. "This isn't right—at all."

"One of the best people that I knew. All of us treasured Honey." I set the book down on the counter and gazed, concerned, at Althea. "Who was that just now? He almost mowed me down and gave me a heart attack."

Althea hesitated for a beat. "Oh, just some loser jerk, and what a piece of work." She wiped away a tear. "You can't please everybody, no matter how you try."

"Well, today was not the day to make his displeasure known. Surely that guy knew what was going on with you, with Honey. What was his problem anyway?"

"A lack of a soul perhaps?" A hard look crossed her eyes. "But enough about the fool. He's taken up enough of my time already."

"Althea," I began, "I'm sure the cops have been here. Have they given any hints about who might have hurt our Honey?" I paused. "Or had she perhaps been ill?" If Honey had been sick, that wasn't information she owed anybody but herself—and perhaps Althea, since they ran the business as a team.

"Honey? Sick? Are you kidding me?" Althea gave me a sad smile. "Girl could do ashtanga yoga, work ten hours in the shop, and then stay up until two a.m. teaching herself French, writing haiku, or whatever. Honey was a force; there was nothing wrong with

Honey." She paused for a moment. "Of course, her life had changed a lot since she moved into the big house with her uncle. So there was not much time for poetry or French."

"So you think that someone…"

"Someone had to, Rue."

"But, Althea, *who?* And why? Do you have any thoughts?"

"I have wracked my brain." Althea turned to the coffee maker and poured us each a cup of her signature honey praline brew. "She never mentioned anybody being mad, but I could tell there was something on her mind over the last few days. She mixed the sugar up with the flour in one of the recipes—which, luckily, I caught. But that was not like Honey. And then…" She took a breath and leaned across the counter. "One day last week, her phone rang, and I just happened to see that it was Archer, the accountant. She talked to him a long time in the back office there. And when she came out of the room, I swear to you it looked like she was about to cry."

Well, now that was interesting. I made a mental note.

"Things okay with the business?"

She slowly sipped her coffee. "Well, I'm not gonna tell you it was the best year ever, but I'm the one who does the books, and we're doing fine. In the black and all of that."

"Maybe it was Carroway Fine Honey that Archer called about. It sounds to me like the uncle needs a lot of help with things he used to do himself."

"Yeah, I think it got to be too much, even for a ball of energy like Honey. Thomas likes to have the business run in a detailed, specific way, and you know how Honey was. Full of fire and spirit, but at heart a people pleaser too. And there were...problem areas, I take it. Not that she said much."

"What problem areas?" I asked.

"There are special products Thomas likes to oversee himself, and he likes to be the one to deal with the accountant. Those jobs are his alone. He seems to be insistent. No ads for the business can go out without Thomas's okay. But with the way his mind is going, a whole lot of that stuff fell into Honey's hands. And Thomas didn't understand why she was taking over."

"What a mess," I said.

"She tried to make him *think* he was in charge, and a lot of time that worked." Althea sighed. "But it was a lot."

"And they could have hired someone!" I sank down into a chair across from the counter. "Or used someone from the staff. Carroway Honey seems to have about a zillion people in their offices downtown."

"He was kind of paranoid, I think. Just in the last year or so. He only trusted Honey, and she was too kind to say no. Family, you know."

Maybe someone didn't like that. Carroway Honey, after all, was raking in a fortune, and maybe someone else wanted that top spot as the confidante of the CEO.

"You said she was distracted," I said to Althea. "Do you think it had to do with Thomas? Or was it something else?" I thought about the bearded guy who was so mad at Althea. If it had to do with business, it was very likely he was furious at Honey too. "That guy who was in—"

Her tone changed in a flash. "No!" she almost shouted. She held up a hand. "Totally unrelated." Then she caught herself and paused. "Hey, look, I'm truly sorry. It's just been a day."

"Of course."

The phone rang, and she picked up. "Spoonful of Honey. Can I help you?"

She listened for a long time. "I thought we had worked that out." She frowned. "Two more, and that is where I'll draw the line, and this time I mean it." I could hear a high-pitched, fevered voice on the other end, but I could not make out the words.

"But we've been over all of that," said Althea with a

sigh, "and I thought we had a deal. Enough is enough, Martin."

Martin. I made a note of the name.

She hung up and rolled her eyes. "People! Rue, I swear to you..." She let her voice trail off.

Then I remembered something. "When I was in yesterday," I said, "Honey seemed to be preoccupied with this little picture on the desk. Like, happy little trees?" I shrugged. "It was kind of cute, but it seemed to...I don't know...upset her for some reason."

I could tell by her expression it didn't ring a bell. "Happy little trees? Well, who even knows with Honey? You know how she was into so many different things. Girl was full of surprises, which is one of the zillion reasons I need Honey in my life."

"Last night when I was in here, Honey seemed just fine. Nothing happened, right? After I left with the food?"

Althea shook her head. We closed soon after that, and she was heading home. You know, to feed her uncle and make sure he was settled before she went to your party." Her voice broke again. "She was so excited when she walked out that door. You know how Honey was— kind of like a kid. A party! And some books! And she was every bit as thrilled as if she were heading to the moon."

We both were quiet for a moment.

"Oh! And she was gonna drop a pie off on her way to the house," said Althea. "It was a key lime pie for Clem Casey's birthday." She gave me a little smile. "No matter what was up with Honey, she'd make a key lime pie— free of charge, of course—and take it over on May 2nd."

I smiled at that. And for the next three weeks, Clem Casey would brag about that pie. In the way of close-knit towns, there were things you could always count on to happen every year. In November, for example, Sarah at the bagel shop would tell us when to expect the cold. When her left knee began to ache, there was a massive scrambling in these parts to find our coats and sweaters.

Then in April—kitten season—little furry faces could be seen peeping through the ties and shirts at Reg's menswear shop until he could find them homes. Soon after that came May and the news from Clem that this year's pie had been—no lie—Honey's best one ever. It was all as much a part of the rhythm of the town as the changing of the seasons.

I checked my phone for the time. "Shoot, I need to run," I said. I had an appointment with a rep for a line of cards I was considering for the shop. I embraced Althea and told her to please let me know if I could do anything for her. Then I headed to the store, where the day got busy with a steady flow of "browsers." Who had come, most likely, more to discuss the news than to purchase books. All of the stores and sidewalks were busier than normal for a Wednesday afternoon in early May. Yet a somber, quiet spirit hovered over all of us as we gathered in small groups, speaking quietly.

Even more than in the other stores, it seemed, my aisles and sitting areas were bustling as the day wore on. The Seabreeze Bookshop had become a hub for the community to gather when there were things to be discussed. With reading nooks, comfy chairs, and selections of fine teas served on vintage china (Elizabeth's idea), I'd worked hard to cultivate a place where readers liked to sit and stay.

Everybody had a theory as rumors were traded in low voices and memories of Honey were quietly discussed. The rumor that persisted most—I heard it several times at least—was that there was someone unexpected in the house last night when Honey arrived home. Other than the usual—Thomas and perhaps one of the staffers.

"That, of course, is who they'll be looking at real hard." Carson from Big Day Out Adventures sat back and crossed one long leg over the other.

"I heard they're at the station being questioned now." Linda from Linda's Alterations raised an eyebrow at the crowd as she sipped her tea.

I made a note to question Andy about this Person X. Not that he would tell me. "Official and confidential business," he would always say—as if I wasn't me, who could be trusted not to blab. People confided quite a lot to the person that they trusted to tell them what to read. I was good at *discreet*.

I had learned, however, not to think too much about the information whispered over tea in the corners of the shop. With my customers, it sometimes became a game to be the "first to know." Tea talk, I had learned, was a lot like the shelves I so carefully curated—a mix of fiction and nonfiction, with an emphasis on the former.

CHAPTER SIX

*T*hat night, I sat out on my big front porch with Andy.

Professional caregivers, he reported, had now been put in place to stay at the mansion round the clock. Andy was among the team conducting interviews, although his private caseload lately seemed to have exploded. "Mostly business stuff," he said. "Partners thinking partners aren't being honest with the books, hiding assets, all of that." He pointed a finger at me. "Family and friends don't mix with business, Rue. I've seen it destroy the closest families, the best relationships. For future reference, please don't ever do that to yourself. It never turns out well. Trust your buddy Andy."

I gave him a look. When he was in detecting mode,

Andy was the best. But the off-duty version sometimes liked to sit down with a whiskey and put his brain in park.

"Andy." I leaned back in my seat and took a sip of my merlot. "Who handed me this business, that, on most days at least, has turned out to be a dream?"

He gave me a sheepish grin. "Well, that would be your gran." He shook his head and chuckled. "And I guess that turned out fine."

I took another sip. "Who is it that I work with almost every single day, to my great delight?"

"That would be Elizabeth, one of your best friends." He held his glass up in a toast. "You, my dear, are the sensational exception to every rule I know." He scratched behind Gatsby's ear. Gatsby was "my" dog unless Andy was around. Then I was summarily ignored. At least I had two cats to snuggle in my lap.

As the two of us grew silent, lost in our own musings, I thought of Honey and Althea. They had come to mind almost right away when Andy gave his warning. Not only were the two of them close friends, they were family as well. I'd forgotten they were cousins—not on the side of the wealthy Carroways, from whom Honey's mother was descended, but on the side of Honey's dad.

"Crooked doings in the business world make for a busy workload for a man such as myself," said Andy. He stared out at the sun, making its exit for the day in a soft mix of gold and red. "But I am all in as well on the death investigation. Top priority. Because if someone hurt our Honey—if it was deliberate what happened to that girl —I am bound and determined that person will be found."

Nobody from the Somerset Harbor Police (at least as far as I knew) had uttered the word "murder." But there was an urgency about their work that told me they weren't thinking accidental death.

"How was your day?" he asked.

"Sad and very long." I took another sip of wine. "Things were busy in the store, and I stopped by to check in on Althea, who, of course, is in a state."

He gave me *that* look. He knew exactly what my reason was to go to Honey's shop. "Rue, you really shouldn't. I can assure you the police have all the bases covered."

"Oh, of course, I know that. I just feel a...*drive* to figure out what happened—to find out for Honey."

"One of our guys was out to the shop as well to speak with Althea." Andy leaned back in his seat. I noticed how his eyes looked tired.

"Any suspects standing out?" I asked him quietly. "Any thoughts on motive?"

He lifted his glass to his lips. "Things are in progress,

Rue. There are several things and several people we are looking at, and we're looking at them hard."

"Like perhaps a bearded man with an axe to grind with Spoonful of Honey or Althea? Who left the store in quite a state?"

"Rue, what do you know?" He looked at me, alert, transformed from drinking buddy into investigator.

"Well, you just told me, Andy, the police sent out a guy, and I had no business there. So I'm sure that you must know every bit as much as I do."

"Rue, if you know something, it's important that you say."

I rubbed Beasley's head. "And does that work both ways?"

He sighed. "Okay, Rue, you win. As long as you go first."

I described the things I had overheard, both from the visitor and from the call that had come in while I was talking with Althea. Oliver pushed his head into my chest, demanding equal head rubs to those I had been giving to his purring brother.

"Interesting," said Andy. "We need to track that guy down right away."

I raised an eyebrow at him. "A tag number, I suppose, might help."

"Are you kidding me?" He gave me a reluctant smile.

"Okay, I'm impressed—and grateful. That will be a help."

"Well, it's just a partial—which I will send you in text." I had it jotted in a little pad I kept in my purse. "Your turn," I told him. "I am hearing there was someone at the house other than the usual—the staff, Honey, and her uncle."

A look of surprise crossed his eyes. "Now, where did you hear that?"

"You hear a lot of things at the Seabreeze the day after an event." I looked him in the eye. "*Was there* a Mr. X, a Mrs. X,—whoever—present at the house?"

"We believe there was, at least for a brief time. Because someone had to come by to bring Honey home." He paused, looking me in the eye. "Just between you and me, Honey's car, it seemed, was missing from the scene."

My hand flew to my mouth. "What do you think that could mean?"

"It's possible someone arrived at the house on foot and fled in Honey's car. Stalking the house, perhaps, which is always something to consider when we're dealing with that kind of wealth." He stared up at the sky, still seeming to consider how it could fit in— Honey's missing car. "But there were no signs of violence," he continued. "And while her uncle is forgetful, surely an intruder would stick in the man's mind. So it is our working theory that—for whatever reason—someone brought her home."

"And you think that person killed her?"

He took a slow sip of his drink. "It's a possibility we must consider, Rue." Andy looked perplexed. "The thing about it is that Althea had assumed Honey had her car at work and drove herself back to the house—as was normally the case. And Honey never said a word about trouble with her car, according to both her sister and Althea."

"And if she got a ride to work and back, that would still beg the question: where is her car now?"

Gatsby stirred and gave a little yip, causing Andy to reach into his pocket for the ever-present treats.

"What did Bea have to say about it?" I asked Andy.

"Well, Bea did express surprise that the car was gone." Andy ran his hand through his thinning hair. "Although, to tell the truth, I'm not sure how much she really knew about her sister's day-to-day." He coughed. "They weren't exactly close, from what I understand."

"What did the others say about it? Uncle Thomas and the staff?"

"None of the staff was there when Honey came back to the house. At least as far as we can tell. It was only Thomas who was home, and, I have to tell you, the information we are getting from Thomas Carroway is...*unreliable.* He simply doesn't have the mental capacity to serve as a proper witness. One minute he is sobbing over Honey's death. And then he will forget altogether what has just occurred. 'My niece will be home soon,' he will say to you. 'You will love my niece.'"

"Very sad," I said. "And to think he's still in charge of Carroway Fine Honey."

"Yeah, Bea is talking now to Stephen Lowry in the downtown offices about having someone step in to see to the day-to-day."

Stephen Lowry. Also on my list of people I should be talking to. His wife Caroline came into the store a lot. She collected cookbooks and also vintage postcards. Now she had every state except Georgia and Ohio. Stephen didn't come in as often as his wife, but on holidays, we always fixed him up with the perfect gifts.

Andy set his glass down. "Well, I should get going. Thank you for the whiskey and the tips."

"Anytime," I said. The drinks were nice, as was the ocean breeze, but these nights on the porch were all about having a companion. Neither of us liked to sit alone with the kinds of thoughts that danced in our heads during times like these.

I stood up and kissed him on the cheek. "Get a good night's rest," I said, "Tomorrow you must rise and shine —and go out and catch a killer."

CHAPTER SEVEN

The next day, my head was spinning as I walked around the block with Gatsby. *Where was Honey's car?*

And also: *Why?* What reason could anybody have to want Honey dead?

Althea, who I just adored, was absolutely hiding something. And then there was Thomas. Honey had been all up in her uncle's business lately. Was Thomas hiding something, and had Honey seen too much? And then there was Bea, who stood now to inherit all of a mega business and not only just the half.

But wait! Bea was Honey's sister; Althea was her best friend, who loved Honey beyond measure. Thomas was the treasured uncle—who'd been Honey's grown-up playmate when she was a little girl. None of those outlandish thoughts made any sense at all.

Oh, but then again, was that not always the way? In every thriller novel, every *Dateline* episode, every lurid headline, it turned out to be the most unlikely person ever.

"They could not have not done it."

How many times had I heard *that* in our True Crime Book Club? As we enjoyed Femme Fatale Fajitas or Murderous Margaritas. (Made, ironically, by Honey, who always had a good time following a theme.)

Questions were still swirling in my mind an hour after that as I caught up on paperwork at the bookshop. Elizabeth and I carried on our business in companionable silence until I heard her calling from across the room: "Aha!"

She looked up at me, a stack of photos in her hand. "When you told me about that parrot at Thomas Carroway's," she said, "I knew there was some connection—something in the family's past that had to do with birds. So I went through my files."

As I made my way over to her, she held up a photo of Charmaine Carroway, the gorgeous ginger-haired mother of three boys. The much-adored youngest had been Thomas. The story went that Thomas was the dreamy, artsy brother who dreamed of a career on stage while the two older brothers were more business-minded. They were the ones who were groomed by their father to take over the already thriving family business.

But when Tim and Teddy Carroway both died in Vietnam, the job fell to the at-first reluctant youngest son. Later, though, the current CEO took to the role with a passion and his own creative bent, working for decades beside his father as the business flourished even more.

Since none of the brothers had children of their own, Carroway Fine Honey was slated to be passed down to Bea and Honey, who were the great-granddaughters of Charmaine's sister Claire.

In the photo, Charmaine gazed out at the camera, her arms outstretched to create a resting place for three elegant white birds.

Cockatoos. A memory was tugging at my mind as well, but it wouldn't fully form.

"Farrah, Freda, and Fiona," Elizabeth told me with a smile. "Back in the day, it seems, Charmaine was pretty famous around town for her exotic birds." She studied the picture too. "Before my time," she said. "Oh, but I've heard stories."

The line of little cockatoos peered placidly at the viewer, proudly showing off the tall crests that sat atop their heads.

"Oh, would you look at them! Like fine little ladies in their best feathered hats," I said, entranced.

Charmaine smiled at the camera in a friendly way, but it was a smile, I noticed, that didn't reach her eyes.

"People say Charmaine never was the same after she lost the boys," mused Elizabeth, "and how could she be? I believe that Tim and Teddy died less than a year apart."

"Well, I hope she found some comfort in her feathered daughters."

"And in her youngest, Thomas. They say the two of them were close, and that they got even closer once the older brothers died. He was a mama's boy, they say. Gave up his big plans to move to Boston after his brothers' deaths. Instead, he stayed in town to learn the business from his father—and see to his mother too. The two of them liked to sail and to spend time in the kitchen creating recipes for Carroway Fine Honey. I have some articles somewhere in the shop about the history of the business. But I do remember that."

That is when it hit me: the memory I couldn't seem to pluck out of my mind—until that very moment. The jars of honey-ginger sauce spilling out of boxes at the mansion—they featured silhouettes of three cockatoos on the yellow labels.

Elizabeth watched me carefully. "Where did you go,

Rue?" She was used to my mind drifting—to some scene from a book, to some random thought.

"Well, it's neither here nor there. But I'm thinking Thomas has been working on a special product—a honey-ginger sauce in honor of his mother," I said to Elizabeth. He had to know his mind was slipping and that he didn't have much time.

"Ginger sauce!" said Elizabeth. "Her husband called her Ginger. Which makes sense, I guess, with those pretty reddish curls."

I told her what I'd seen at the mansion.

She let out a sigh. "Isn't it so sad when your dreams last longer than the ability of your mind to keep up?" She began straightening some photos. "Any news from Andy on the investigation?"

"Yes! He told me yesterday that Honey's car is missing! But, at least for now, that's just for us to know."

Elizabeth stared at me. "I don't understand. How did she get home?"

"No one seems to know!" In my mind, I replayed my conversation with Althea. Althea never mentioned any trouble with the used BMW Honey always loved and treated with such care. Then I thought of something else. "You know, Elizabeth, Althea said that Honey dropped off a key lime pie that night to Clem Casey and his wife. So she had to have her car!"

"Unless she called an Uber."

"Well, yes, I suppose." Ideas turned in my mind, then I thought, "Of course." I knew who I had to ask. "Could you keep an eye on things while I run out to see the Caseys?" An order had come in for Helen, so there was my excuse. Since she and Clem didn't like to drive as much now that they were getting older, I could drop it by while I was "out and about." I special-ordered large-print books for Helen and some of our other older readers, who sometimes had to wait a little longer to dive in to the new, buzzworthy books.

"Go for it." Elizabeth waved me away. "I'll be here organizing and looking through some ideas Bea sent for my new den." My friend rolled her eyes. "Although I think she may have mistaken me for a Rockefeller. I really need to bring her down a notch with this. I don't think my budget fits the kinds of rooms Bea likes to design." She took in a breath. "Oh, but don't you love *this?*" She pulled out a photo of a deep green couch with oversized throw pillows in gold and maroon.

"I could take a nice, long nap on *that,*" I said. It looked both elegant and comfy.

"Bea does have exquisite taste. I will give her that."

"You know, Elizabeth, you do deserve a splurge."

"I do! And do you know what I think I'll do? I think

I'll buy a couch." Elizabeth whipped out her phone. "Let me call her now before I change my mind."

I gave her a thumbs-up as I went behind the desk and grabbed the historical romances reserved for Helen Casey.

CHAPTER EIGHT

he Caseys lived in a neat brick home at the edge of town. Helen had taken up roses as a hobby in her retirement years, and blooms in red and yellow seemed to welcome me from the flower bed. I parked in the street in front of their house, and I made my way down their walkway.

No need to ring the bell, as Clem's round face popped up in a window before I reached the stoop. A welcoming grin was spread across his features, although it was more subdued than the hardy enthusiasm with which he normally greeted friends and even strangers. Clem was the retired Director of Tourism for our town, and he was quite the extrovert—a true people person. For that reason, I suspected retirement had not been easy on him. Helen, on the other hand, was the quiet type who loved to lose herself in her gardening and her books.

"What a nice surprise," he said, throwing the door open. "Once word gets out that a man has the world's best key lime pie sitting in his kitchen, his doorbell gets a workout."

Helen was right behind him. "Oh, Rue." She noticed the books in my hand. "You are way too kind to your customers. We don't drive that much—cataracts, you know—but one of our daughters could have surely brought me into town." Her gray hair fell in soft curls just above her shoulders, and her eyes were filled with gratefulness.

"Well, I was coming right this way, and you have some good ones. I thought you might be anxious to dive right into these."

"And here is your reward." Clem cut an extra-large slice of pie and brought it to the table while his wife rushed to the coffee maker.

"Dear, do you take cream?" she asked.

"Please. I don't mean to impose," I said. "Just dropping by the books." But Helen and I both knew Clem craved the company. And I, of course, was itching for some information (and wouldn't mind some pie).

Soon, we were seated around the table. "It would be

impolite to let you eat alone," Clem said as he dug his fork into his slice.

Tears filled Helen's eyes as our minds immediately went to the maker of the pie. "Such a thoughtful girl," my hostess said. "So young—her whole life ahead of her." She set down her fork, unable to take a bite.

"Such a mystery." I took a sip of coffee. "On the night it happened, I was in her shop." I paused. "She seemed a little stressed. But she basically was Honey—looking forward to her trip and to my party at the store." I glanced from Clem to Helen. "Did you get the idea she was worried? Like that she was being threatened. Or in danger? Anything at all?"

"Well, I do think that her uncle was heavy on her mind." Helen let out a sigh. "We asked how things were going—you know, with his health. And how it was for her living at his house. And she got *very* quiet—like Honey almost never did."

"Always had a lot to say." Clem stuffed another bite of pie into his mouth.

"And I just got the idea she didn't want to go there, so I simply changed the subject," Helen said.

Clem raised an eyebrow at me. "Word has gotten round to us that Thomas isn't well. But back in the day, the man was really something. He was a force of nature, always with an eye to business." He forked up his last bite of pie. "I remember one day he paid me a little visit back when I had Clem's Market, my little store in town. I had begun to carry upscale condiments and sweets— some of my own creation—and he did not take well to that." He put down his fork. "That part of the business was starting to take off. People liked my stuff so much I was shipping out of state to the friends and family of my local customers. And Thomas seemed to think I was stepping on his turf." He sighed. "So I concentrated more on breads and meats and still did fairly well. But I could have been a sauce man! If I had stood my ground."

"Oh, darling, let it go." Helen gently grabbed his hand. "That was a hundred years ago. You were both young men."

"Then once he started pulling in the millions, some of those products he was selling looked familiar to me, if you get my drift."

"Well, you both found your paths," said Helen soothingly. "While it takes good products to make a company, it was the family legacy that made Thomas his real money. Clem's was a special store, but promoting our town to the world is what you were meant to do."

"No ill will to Thomas." Clem waved a hand in the air. "I had a job I loved; I helped a lot of people, and I have a little nest egg to hand over to my girls. What more could I want? And there may be a little something coming to me from Thomas Carroway, I'd guess, when he passes from this world—as a little thank you for my 'inspiration' when it came to those sauces."

"Did you know," asked Helen, "that Clem and Thomas played on the Somerset Harbor Razorbills when they went undefeated two years in a row? A historic year! And they were the best of friends."

"I pitched and he played third base. And let me tell you, Rue, that man was *on fire* out there in the outfield. Lots of our opponents met their defeat at third," Clem said with a smile.

Our town was immensely proud of its amateur baseball league.

My eyes wandered to the backyard, where I could see more expansive gardens through the kitchen window. At the edge of the drive, Clem's red truck was parked next to Helen's Lexus, neither of which, I imagined, had seen much use in recent months.

And—my heart skipped a beat—*there was Honey's BMW right behind the Lexus.* I leaned forward to be sure. The car was nearly hidden behind the oversized branches of an oak.

"Honey's car!" I said. "Why is her car here?"

Helen glanced at Clem, and Clem glanced at Helen.

Helen stood up from the table and began to clear the dishes. "Poor girl's car just wouldn't crank. She was so upset. Clem offered to go out there and have a look for her."

"I know a thing or two about automotives," said her husband. "But it got Honey feeling anxious. She said she had things to do, places that she had to be."

Helen met my eyes. "Rue, she was so excited about that party you were having. She wanted to make sure she got to your store."

"So how did Honey get home?"

"She called her sister," Helen said.

Just as if the answer was as simple as that.

CHAPTER NINE

I called Andy from the car and put the call on speakerphone as I pulled out onto the street.

"Rue." He picked up right away. "There's been a...*development*, let's say, with Thomas Carroway. We're scrambling over here, so I only have a moment."

"What development?" I asked.

"I've been speaking with the maid. There were words, apparently, between Honey and her uncle not long before she died. Very heated words. As in he accused his niece of undermining...how did he put it, now? Of undermining what he called the 'crowning glory' of his time in business. His final legacy for Carroway Fine Honey. His *pièce de résistance,* he said."

"Well, that's some fancy praise for honey-ginger sauce."

"Honey-ginger sauce?" He paused. "Rue, what do *you* know that I don't? According to the maid, Thomas Carroway was livid."

"Did Thomas make a threat? I know how bad it sounds. But listen to me, Andy. You need to look at *Bea*. Because, Andy, here's the thing…"

"Rue, we have discussed this. I am well aware the sisters had their issues, but I really need to go. In addition to the thing with Thomas, we're trying to track down who may have taken Honey home that night. Crucial information! And it's been assigned to me to contact anyone I can in regard to that."

"But, Andy…"

"Lyft, Uber, cabs. I have to call them all. As well as any merchants near Honey's place of business who might have surveillance footage that could help. Roger Eaton called in sick this morning with a hundred degrees of fever. Strep throat's going round. So it all falls to me."

Sheesh. Andy, take a breath! He had someone on the phone with the answer now. No more calls would be required.

"A good investigator, Andy, knows when to drop the questions and *listen* for the answer." I paused. "It was Bea. It was Bea who picked her up."

A stunned silence filled the car, then he let out a breath. "You have my attention. Talk."

I described my visit with the Caseys and their stunning revelation. "Neither Clem nor Helen saw Bea's car arrive," I said, "but Honey said she thought her sister could swing by. And soon after that, her phone buzzed and out the door went Honey."

"That changes everything," said Andy. "Bea seemed stunned to learn Honey's car was not outside at the mansion—which means Bea is hiding something." He paused to clear his throat. "Thank you for that, Rue, and now I *really* have to go. I need to inform the chief—and then major change of plans."

I stopped for a light. "I guess you will be going to the service in the morning."

"Pick you up at the store? Then we can go for lunch. I owe you a lobster roll for investigative work. Quite the development."

"With fries and dessert—and you'll be getting off real cheap."

I heard murmurs in the background, then he called to someone. "Be right there," he told them before returning to the call. "See you at a quarter till." It was the rushed tone of a man who had things to do.

The next day, the Presbyterian Church in town was packed. I had closed the store for the service and lunch hour since Elizabeth, Jana, and I all wanted to pay our respects to Honey.

Beside me, Andy glanced around, both as a grieving friend and an investigator. I knew perpetrators often showed their faces at funerals and wakes. They sometimes acted rather strangely, setting themselves apart. Which is why the cops might be on hand when the victim of a murder's laid to rest. My mysteries and true-crime paperbacks had taught me a thing or two.

But in this case, of course, it looked like the guilty party might be right up there in front in the family pew —which still blew my mind. On the walk over to the church, Andy had given me an update. He and the chief had spoken once again to Bea not long after my call. And not only had she denied picking up her sister; she had accused the cops of "gross incompetence" and acting on reports from "lying witnesses," allowing her sister's killer to walk free.

"In the hours before your party, she claims she was home taking care of client billing," he explained. "So, conveniently, there is no one to confirm or deny her alibi. Today's plan includes canvassing her neighbors to see if one of them might have witnessed her blue Lexus coming or going from her drive."

Soft organ music signaled the service was beginning, and we settled in to listen. In addition to the pastor, several friends of Honey spoke, including one with whom she volunteered to wash dogs in order to raise money for the animal shelter here.

"I didn't know she ever did that," I whispered to Andy. "She never said a word." I also learned that Honey was ranked nationally in tennis when she was a high school senior and that she had planned a list of quirky sites for her trip to Scotland. "Who puts first on their itinerary an ancient house with a pineapple on the top?"

"What the heck?" mouthed Andy.

Oh, yes, that was Honey. Skip the mountain vistas and the castles, and go directly to the humongous pineapple that towered—forty feet tall—on the roof of an old home. Dating back, apparently, to when the fruit was an exotic treat for the well-to-do.

I suppressed a giggle (Honey would approve) but also felt the urge to weep over all the stories I'd never hear her tell.

"She surprised us every day," said one friend with a smile. She then explained how Honey had taught the parrot how to sing the pop song called "Too Sexy." And just before a meeting between Uncle Thomas and an advertising rep.

I tried to imagine Thomas's surprise when the bird burst into song. *I'm too sexy for my hat...*

A soft spattering of laughter could be heard among the crowd.

My eyes went to the front, where Bea was supporting the distraught family patriarch. On the other side, an unknown man held his other arm. Then my attention moved several rows behind them, where a young woman, a petite blonde, was shaking in her grief. The man beside her reached to stroke her arm, and she lay her head on his shoulder, overcome. Several times as the pastor and friends spoke, her sobs had carried back to where I sat with Andy near the rear of the church.

She might be extended family, I decided. From the back, in fact, this woman could be Honey minus the green streak in her hair. And she sat in a line of mourners in which Althea was included. These must be the Lindstroms, the working-class side of Honey's family.

Two rows behind this group, Paul Budd sat alone with his head in his hands. I wondered how serious things might have become between Paul and Honey. He was on my list to talk to: Paul Budd, the accountant, Stephen Lowry from the downtown office of Carroway Fine Honey...

When Andy nudged my arm, I noticed that my mind

had wandered. The service apparently had ended, and the family was exiting their pews. When a few others began to slowly make their way into the aisles in the hushed atmosphere, Andy nodded to the door. "What do you say we beat the crowd to the Seafood Shack?" he asked.

I blinked away a tear and nodded, then we were on our way.

CHAPTER TEN

I sunk my teeth into the buttery bread and sweet lobster meat. "So, what's next?" I asked. A crowd of mourners was crammed into the entranceway, waiting for more tables to be cleared.

Andy's phone had been glued to his ear for most of our lunch as he caught up on a stream of updates from the station.

"Bea has lawyered up, it seems," he told me quietly. He set down his phone and picked up his lobster roll. "We'd love to get our hands on her phone and her computer too, see what stories they might tell." He took a bite and seemed to ponder as he chewed.

I had yet to get over being stunned that the evidence was pointing to Honey's sister of all people. But if she hadn't done it, why would Bea have lied to the cops about picking Honey up that night and taking her back home?

"It's looking bad for Bea." Andy continued to keep his voice very quiet. "But who really knows what was going on with that family, Rue? The involvement of one person does not always preclude the involvement of another." He took a bite of lobster roll. "Or Bea could have brought Honey home and seen something that she'd rather the whole world not know. And *that* might have been the reason that she lied to us that night."

I reached over with a napkin to wipe a bit of butter from his chin. "Like, she'd protect her *sister's killer* to protect the family name? To protect Carroway Fine Honey?"

"All I can tell you, Rue, is that money seems to be a motivator when it comes to Bea. Cash flow, profits, all of that, is what the woman worships."

"Are there signs the business wasn't thriving as we thought?" I thought about how shaken Honey was after her phone call with Archer Fancher, the accountant.

"Yes, in fact there are," he told me quietly. "Profits are way down, although nobody really knows that except Thomas and a few of his top people. He was very secretive, it seems, even more so than we knew."

A chill ran through my core. "And maybe Honey found out. Maybe Honey got too close." I closed my eyes. Suddenly, it was all too much, my thoughts of her last hours. "Call me naive, Andy, but I *have* to think someone who knew Honey could not have...ended things."

I thought about the nights I'd dropped in at the mansion to pick Honey up for dinner or a movie when a staffer could stay late to make sure her uncle was okay. A scene flashed in my mind: Honey gently singing Beatles songs to her frail Uncle Thomas while she made sure he ate his soup. I saw Bea and Honey together in my store as Honey teased a smile from her no-nonsense sister—as only she could do.

Andy raised an eyebrow as he took a sip of coffee. "But it was you yourself who turned us on to the fact that Bea is lying through her teeth about what she did that night."

I looked down at my plate, no longer one bit hungry. I wanted just to go home, take the whole day off, and lose myself in a book. Those worlds in the pages would be *so* much better than this screwed-up version of real life. That should be my motto at the Seabreeze—*Shop! Get lost! Escape!*

"So, you never finished telling me what Thomas said to Honey—about what the maid told you. You know, about the threat?" Back to the real world I went; I owed that to Honey.

It was the story he had started on the phone when I cut in to tell him about Bea and the ride home.

"Oh, yeah." Andy frowned and scratched behind his ear. "It was kind of bad. The uncle accused Honey of 'bringing ruination down on the family business.' He called her a traitor, Rue."

"Do you think it was the illness?" Clearly Thomas Carroway was half out of his mind.

"The man is clearly ill. But as long as she has worked for him, cleaning that big house, Sally Densley knows the man as well as anyone." Andy cleared his throat. "What Sally said to me is that Thomas has his good days, when his mind is very clear. The night he lit into Honey, he knew what he was saying, and he meant what he said. Or so Sally believes."

"And, Andy, when was this?"

"The same week Honey died."

Something curdled in my stomach.

Andy wiped his mouth. "Apparently, he understood he didn't have much time, and he had one more project to complete before stepping down from his position. It was his opinion that Honey was interfering in a big way with this grand idea of his."

"But what idea was that?"

Andy shook his head and frowned. "That is the big question. Thomas claims no memory of what he said to Honey. And no one on his staff was familiar with the project or the product or whatever." He leaned forward in his seat. "What were you saying on the phone, Rue... about a honey-ginger sauce? Do you think that could be it?"

I told him about the closet full of sauce jars, the only hint of disarray in a carefully ordered house.

Still, something didn't fit. We sat in silence for a while as my eyes roamed the other tables, mostly filled with families. And that is when it hit me. "The sauces were created in honor of *his mother*," I told Andy. That was the part that didn't fit. A man whose final wish was centered on the woman he had cooked with and adored as a child surely couldn't be the killer. That same man would never kill his loving niece to bring that wish to fruition. Or perhaps he could; perhaps the world was more heartbreaking than I thought.

I explained to Andy how Elizabeth's portal to the past had given me some insights into his relationship with Charmaine Carroway. "And that is why that sauce was so important to him."

"But apparently it needed more honey or more ginger or whatever." Andy leaned back in his seat. "The stuff did not appear to be flying off the shelves."

"Or perhaps they ran out of the funds to promote it?" Or maybe the sauce was not his own. Clem still seemed to hold on to some anger about the "borrowing" of recipes that ended up in jars labeled Carroway.

Andy sighed. "What we do know is the sauce mattered to Thomas a great deal, and he could have seen it as a key to holding up the good name of the family and the business." He looked at me intently. "And who else would share that motive?"

The money-loving sister.

Then his phone dinged with a message, and we both sat up straight. He picked it up and listened briefly before setting down his phone. "Well, it's official now. There was poison in her system. Somebody poisoned Honey."

That empty mug I'd seen at the mansion. Had a final sip of something sparkling or sweet caused Honey's heart to stop?

"That mug," I said. "I'm sure you saw it, Andy."

"It had the fingerprints of Thomas Carroway. And except for Honey's prints, they were the only ones."

Honey had told me once she and her uncle had a ritual of ending each night with toddy. She'd put a cinnamon-chocolate stirrer in the honey-whiskey mix as a fun little garnish—and a pre-bedtime snack. It helped ease Uncle Thomas, she explained, into a restful state as she told him stories from the past, taking him back to a time he was on top of his game, when more of the family was alive to fill the house with laughter.

It made for a nice picture—or a tragic one.

CHAPTER ELEVEN

The whole town seemed to be in mourning the day the family buried Honey Lindstrom in a private ceremony following the service at the church. Some of the regulars stopped in at the store to pick up sweet romances, humorous books of essays, whatever got them through. I noticed a few of the other stores had a steady stream of customers as well, despite the air of respectful quiet that hung above the sidewalks. Everyone, it seemed, was turning to their favored forms of comfort: silk scarves, Tylenol, a fine chablis with notes of pear and citrus... I imagined those were among the items tucked into the shopping bags I saw on shoppers' arms.

A dog's cold nose against your face was also good, I thought, as Gatsby came to nuzzle me while I finished some reports. The sun peeking through the window made me long for some fresh air, so I grabbed Gatsby's leash. The customers had cleared out for the moment, and I told Elizabeth I would be right back.

Gatsby's steps grew quicker when he figured out we were heading to the little park at the edge of downtown. Honey had confided to me once she had a favorite bench, the one closest to the lake. It was away from a lot of the action, and it had a view of the Dotted Hawthorn with its delicate white flowers with the small white dots.

"It's so quiet there," she had said.

"You don't strike me as the type who would go for quiet," I had told her on that day. "You're the kind who seems to thrive on having people all around." As opposed to me, who liked to sit for hours with my books.

"Oh, I do love people. I love to soak them in, hear what they have to say." She'd paused. "I take a lot of pride in being a good listener. But sometimes I need to sit and listen to *myself.*"

I thought of that conversation as I settled down on Honey's bench, hoping that could somehow bring me closer to my friend. Her Hawthorn tree was in bloom, I noted, and there was just a hint of wind to stir the branches and the water; she would have liked this day.

An older woman sat nearby with her knitting. She

watched me carefully as I wiped away a tear. "Must be a friend of Honey's?" she asked me in a whisper.

"I was kind of hoping I could feel her in this place."

The woman made a careful stitch. "Honey loved that bench, and I come here a lot as well. I think we both respected each other's need for quiet. But if I was feeling low, Honey sensed that too. She knew when to let me be and when I needed her to ask about the pain in my left knee." She stared out at the lake. "Or the darkness that sometimes overcomes me since my husband passed."

I nodded. I imagined it could sometimes be elusive, the quiet Honey craved. She drew people to her; they seemed to seek her out.

The woman seemed to read my mind. "And sometimes she'd just nod, and that was all I needed on that afternoon—to just feel less alone."

I wiped away another tear, and we sat in silence for a while as Gatsby napped against my feet. A goldfinch topped a branch and turned its head to lick its wings, and I allowed my thoughts to wander.

"I hope they catch that girl," said the woman, pain catching in her voice.

"*That girl?*" My heart skipped a beat.

"The kind of nasty one. The one with the pink hair."

Althea?

"I don't understand." I sat up straight, alert.

"I saw them arguing. A week ago, it must have been. Oh, yes, it was last Wednesday, because I came here that day with my slice of apple pie—apple pie with cheddar. Which is my treat on Wednesdays when the desserts go on special at Your Slice of Pie. Otherwise, I can't afford it. Those retirement dollars don't stretch the way they should."

"That sounds like Honey's partner. But what were they arguing about?" I asked.

"Hmph. 'Partner,' did you say? She wasn't much of one. The things she said to Honey! That Honey ruined everything, which was ridiculous, of course. If anything was 'ruined,' it wasn't Honey's fault; I am sure of that. Although I have no idea what this crazy woman was going on about." My new confidante looked me in the eye. "But I will tell you, dear, it just broke my heart, the hurt on Honey's face." My companion shook her head.

My heart was pounding now.

"Do you know, specifically, what Honey might have done that had Althea so worked up? That is her name —Althea."

"She was just shouting nonsense as far as I could tell." The woman paused to think. "I did hear her say she had always *trusted* Honey and that was no longer true. Everything had changed, according to this woman, who was, frankly, being rude. They weren't all that close to me," she added. "They were over there, near where I like to park." She nodded to her right. "But this Althea was so loud." She picked back up with her knitting. "So much for quiet time, which I imagined Honey had come here to find."

Everything had changed—and some of the customers at the women's business seemed to be unhappy, even livid. What was going on? And, most importantly, how far had Althea gone to make things "right" again?

Althea—although I hated to admit it—seemed to have both means and motive. The two partners in the business had loved to taste whatever treat the other might have been cooking up. It would have been pretty simple for Althea to slip in a little something extra to "solve" whatever problem she might have had with Honey.

So many possibilities—and every one of them absolutely broke my heart. Everybody close to Honey seemed to be hiding something.

CHAPTER TWELVE

*T*hings stayed quiet at the store with a few customers settling into the reading nooks with their tea and fictional escapes. Oliver went from customer to customer nuzzling their shins while Beasley watched them warily from behind the display of stationery. It was a favorite spot for him because of the basket underneath filled with cozy throws. The throws, of course, were meant to have been put away—not a summer item—but they had become a soft place for a small, shy cat to hide, and so they remained. We were all about comfort at the bookshop—for our readers and our furry family alike.

The words blurred on the screen as I perused some of the buzz-worthy titles scheduled for release. But my mind would not be still enough to decide on any orders. In the end, I just gave up on trying to fix my thoughts on anything but Honey. I slipped into my office, hoping— fingers crossed—I could get ahold of Andy. I had been trying frequently since I got back from the park.

As usual, his tone sound rushed—and a bit irritated. "I know you're worried, Rue, and I promise I will call you if there's any news that I am free to share."

"Or maybe I have news," I said.

He paused. "I'll admit that you've lucked out with some things that have turned out to be a tremendous help. But I really need to—"

Whoa. What did he just say? "It was more *work* than *luck*, but I will let that go, because this afternoon, I learned—"

"Rue, I've told you that we've got this." Then his voice grew soft. "Investigative work can be a dangerous endeavor to get yourself involved in. And whoever did that thing to Honey might go to any lengths to keep somebody's mouth shut if they find out too much. Which is why I beg of you: leave the sleuthing to the pros."

"I wasn't sleuthing, Andy." This time, I really wasn't. "I just went to the park. And I thought you'd like to know that Honey had a blowup with Althea the week before she died. Althea yelled at Honey, said Honey ruined *something*, that she could no longer even trust her."

"*What?*"

I carefully explained.

There was quiet on the line, and I knew that Andy—much like I had done—was trying to puzzle out what the heck was going on at Somerset Harbor's favorite caterer.

"Hey, did you ever manage to track down that guy—who left Spoonful of Honey in a huff?"

"Benson Francis," Andy said. "Owns Francis's Cigars on Baylor Street in town."

"Oh, yeah. I've heard the name."

"He told me Honey and Althea's place did his daughter's wedding, and the food wasn't up to par. Things were not as promised. But, Rue, I got the feeling there was something else, something that the man didn't want to say. Nobody gets that hot over chicken breasts that are overcooked or too much spice in the little sausage balls."

"Hmm."

"Said he dealt with Althea, who refunded him his money, and he said that was that."

"Hmm."

"Rue." There was a warning in his voice. "Don't you go over there."

The thing was, I really should. If Andy's gut was saying that the man was withholding information, it might be up to me to pull it out of him. People told me things; they confided in me. Even strangers. I had come to recognize it as one of my superpowers.

Or maybe first I'd go find Paul at his smoothie place. It could be that Honey had confided in her man, and maybe he would talk to me since Paul and I were friends. And I was a customer as well. Sometimes a smoothie on a hot day could be just the thing. And, if I remembered right, this was one of the days he was at the store in town. He tried to spend some time at each of the stores he owned to get to know the locals.

"Just passing on the info," I told Andy breezily. "And I will let you go since it's busy, busy there. I think maybe I'll run out and pick up some smoothies for Elizabeth and me." Then maybe I would check out some cigars— but of course I didn't say that to Mr. "Leave it All to Me."

I stepped back up to the front and straightened a display of beach-themed reads. Tiny beach umbrellas were interspersed among the books, stuck in little glasses filled with sand.

A young woman slowed down as she passed the

table. "Erin Hilderbrand!" She picked up a paperback, excited. "I've always loved her stuff."

I glanced down at her choice. "And that one's really good." Several other books were stacked in a basket at the woman's feet. I glanced at the titles. "You have good taste, I see. Looks like you're stocking up."

"Well, I always say, why come to the beach if you can't sit with a stack of books and let the waves run across your feet?"

A man appeared beside her. "Well, you *could* come to the beach to surf. Or maybe to swim?" He rolled his eyes, and she laughed.

"That's your thing, not mine." She handed him her basket. "Why don't you pay for these while I get us some tea."

"If you're ready," I told him, "I can help you up in front."

"I am just the man with the credit cards," he teased as he followed me.

As I rang up the books, his eyes moved to the photo of me and Honey that I'd framed on a whim and put beside the register just the day before. We were at a barbecue, and I was laughing with my eyes closed at something she'd just said. Honey stared directly at the camera with that Honey smile.

"Daughter? Sister?" he asked me.

They must be out-of-towners, I decided. Most people here knew Honey, and if they didn't know her, they'd surely seen her picture in the paper over the past week.

"Just a dear, dear friend," I said.

"Crazy coincidence," he said, "but I saw that girl yesterday when we went out to eat. We were at Eggs Galore, and I had to turn around when I heard that girl's laugh. It was, like, contagious, and I wanted to know so badly what could be that funny."

I paused, my hand in mid-air, with my fingers poised to hit the register. That *did* sound like Honey. Was she sending me a sign that she was okay?

"Cool friend that you have," he said. "She put peanut butter and honey on her bagel, which was kind of brilliant, really. Who's to say she has to eat her bagel like everybody else?"

This was feeling weird. Because that as well was so very much like Honey. Always an ambassador for the family product. Put honey in your bath, honey in your veggies, and did you know that honey was good for that sore throat?

I managed a smile as I handed him the books. "I hope your wife enjoys these, and that you get in some surfing while she reads."

He gave me a thumbs-up.

I sank down on my stool as his wife brought him his tea and they exited the store with their drinks packaged up to go. I glanced across the room at Elizabeth. "You look like a woman who could use a smoothie," I called out to her.

She smiled. "That would be delightful, Rue."

CHAPTER THIRTEEN

*J*uice It Up was a quick two blocks away, and Gatsby, as always, was elated to be out and about among his people. He was quite the celebrity, my dog. Becky at the butcher's stuck her head out to scratch him behind the ears. Reg, who was outside straightening a sales rack, greeted the big dog like one of his best buds.

I, in turn, smiled down at his calico cat, Marie, who was napping in the sun. The pets on this day were giving all of us a reason to focus on something other than our common tragedy.

I loved it that my dog had become so well loved in town. When I had first arrived, my shyness had sometimes threatened to get the best of me, but it was not that way with Gatsby, and he'd helped to insert me firmly into the heart of the town. Everyone he met was Gatsby's new best friend—well, almost everyone. Gatsby had a radar when it came to people, and he was never, ever wrong.

Hmm. Perhaps I should take a closer look at his reactions to Bea and Thomas and Althea.

Soon, we had made our way to Juice It Up, where the door was standing open to let in the early summer breeze. Like many of the local merchants, Paul kept treats on hand for pets. As we walked inside, he came out from around the counter with a banana slice topped with peanut butter. He presented it to Gatsby, who thanked him with a happy bark before gobbling down the treat in a single bite.

Paul bent down toward the dog. "Your friend Rue will have to pay for her treat today, but it's on the house for you. Who's my favorite boy?" he cooed, rubbing Gatsby's neck.

"He loves being spoiled, and I think you've made his day," I said with a smile. Then my eyes turned serious as I gazed at Paul. "Paul, how in the world are you? I just can't imagine." I gave him a look that was full of meaning. "Honey let me know you two were going out."

As happened every time, I was struck right away with one of the main reasons the Somerset Harbor women were such big fans of smoothies. While the drinks were fresh and fabulous, they might not have been the main attraction here. The owner was the kind of gorgeous that could take your breath away. Paul had chiseled features and sincere dark eyes that seemed to see directly into the deepest part of you.

"It still just seems unreal." He leaned against the counter. "I want to fix it somehow, to jump back into last week and warn her—or protect her." He let out a sigh. "I want to *fix it*, Rue, but I can't bring Honey back. Our Honey is just...gone, which isn't right at all."

"And the cops think someone *did it*, as opposed to something with her health or an accident or something." I let out a sigh. "Did she say anything to you about any kind of trouble? Because it just seems beyond me that anyone would..." I let my voice trail off.

He rubbed his hands under the dispenser of hand sanitizer on the counter. "Well, her uncle's health was bad, and he could be difficult, as she might have shared with you. But Honey made it work. Ever since she was a child, I think, she had loved that man." He looked down at the floor and frowned. "But there was something else, something I could tell was really eating at her. Like, one time during dinner, she just burst into tears. And I asked her, 'Honey, *what?*' But she changed the subject every time. Said our time together was her time to be happy.

So I tried to, you know, not pepper her with questions, to just show her a good time."

"Was everything okay between Honey and Althea? And between her and Bea?" I hardly knew which person I should start with; things were that complicated.

"I did overhear one phone call where things got a little tense between her and Althea. Something that had to do with…ginger-honey sauce? I do remember that. Because it got the wheels in my mind kind of rolling about a new flavor we could do for a summer smoothie. But mainly because Honey looked so sad that night. And that was a night that had started out so well. I had made cucumber-mint mojitos, and we took them to the beach just as the sun was setting." He shook his head and sat down at an empty table. "I really wanted that night to be special for us. But it was like a light in her went out after she got that call. And I kind of felt that light was in my care, but I couldn't get it back. She was somehow changed in that last week or so." His mind looked far away, lost in some memory.

The honey-ginger sauce again! Why was she fighting with *Althea* about the special sauce that was part of the honey business and not the catering, which had always been a separate thing?

"Did she ever mention Bea?"

"She did tell me Bea had come around the mansion

more than usual over the last few weeks. Which Honey thought was good—you know, for the sake of their Uncle Thomas." He let out a sigh. "With Bea, you always wonder, though, if there is another motive. You know— aging uncle, family fortune, all of that. But I always hoped for Honey's sake that Bea had more of a heart for family than it might appear." His eye moved to the door. "Rue, let me get your order before this group comes in. It looks like a big one."

A knot of about ten girls, who looked like they were in high school, waved to Paul and giggled as they made their way to the counter. Some of his fan club had arrived.

I ordered a mango smoothie for Elizabeth and a creamy avocado smoothie for myself, which Paul fixed quickly and efficiently.

"Again, Paul, I'm really sorry," I told him in a whisper.

"Well, we had something special, and I'll hold on to that. And parts of her life were good right up to the end. Last week, I heard her laughing so hard with her sister, laughing till they cried."

Well, that was nice to hear. "Sometimes I think there's more to Bea than we give her credit for," I said.

"Oh, no! Her *other* sister." Paul gave me a wink. "About Bea I'm not so sure."

"Her…wait a minute. *What?*"

He glanced at the line, which had grown even longer with more high school girls. "Come back soon," he said. "I'd love to talk some more with someone else who loved Honey."

"But what did you mean when you…"

One of the girls, though, was already giving him her order for the strawberry-mango special.

I was somewhat in a daze as I pulled my dog away from his cooing teenage fans. Then we were on our way, my mind a whirl of questions.

I took Elizabeth her drink and passed the last hours at the store straightening displays, answering some emails, and trying to puzzle out what was up with that bombshell from Paul. Andy didn't pick up, but I doubted even he could have known a thing like that and kept that information from me.

When the day at last dragged to an end, I left my car in the lot and began to walk the six blocks home with Gatsby. I was feeling anxious, and maybe exercise would help. As a confidante of Honey's, I felt duty-bound to find the answer, but each clue seemed to bring a barrage of other questions, taking me further from the answer than when I had started out.

I noticed as I passed through town that a few stores were open late, catering to the crowds who filled the sidewalks in the evenings, enjoying the restaurants and the bars. Luckily—and perhaps as a sign—it just so happened one of those shops with the lights still on was Francis's Cigars.

A classical-sounding chime announced our arrival as Gatsby and I stepped onto the plush carpet. Benson Francis looked up from his laptop at the rear of the store, giving me a pleasant smile. He was alone in the store except for the quiet company of a wooden Indian. But then I looked again, and there was someone else. A friendly-looking Dalmatian seemed to welcome us as well from beside the owner's desk.

"Welcome! Can I help you?" Benson didn't seem to recognize me from our near collision at Spoonful of Honey, which was just as well. I wanted to appear as just a random stranger to whom he might open up. I needed him to talk about his daughter's wedding, the reception that came after, and what in the world it was that had gone so very wrong. I suspected he was not alone with whatever problem had sent him into such a red-faced furor. In the short time I was there, Althea took another call that also seemed to be from an enraged client. *I thought we had worked that out...enough is enough.*

"Oh, my goodness, yes, I will need lots of help," I told Benson with a laugh. "I don't know the first thing, I'm afraid, about buying a cigar, but I need a special gift."

"Well, then I would be your man." He rose from his seat. "Even before cigars became my line of work, cigars were my passion. Nothing like a fine cigar to end the day on a peaceful note, to bond one friend or family member to another. Your recipient, I think, will be very pleased—and also very lucky—you thought of a cigar."

This guy knew how to sell. I should take some notes.

"It's for my son-in-law," I said. "Or *future* son-in-law —who is just the best. We've all been in a state, getting ready for the wedding. So many decisions to be made. Venue, flowers, music—although, of course, I know no wedding can be perfect. But I am trying very hard to make it special for them both. Always complications! We'd picked a caterer, and then...oh, my! I suppose you've heard about the *murder*." I said it in a quiet, solemn tone to mark the tragedy it was.

The dog in the back whined a little, as if in sympathy.

"Just horrific," Benson said.

"And we had worked the menu out so nicely. One thing all taken care of! And the food, I've heard, is just divine from Spoonful of Honey." Then I paused and shook my head. "But would you listen to me? I'm ashamed! Going on and on about my *food*, while that poor girl has died. And I'm sure our guests will still be enamored with the dinner and the cake and all the rest. The other partner has assured me she will carry on—

with the same quality ingredients, the same recipes. Spoonful of Honey will go on!"

"Um..." He crossed his arms and stared down at the floor.

When he hesitated, I cocked my head at him, encouraging him to go on with what he'd like to say.

"I have never been a man to speak ill of the dead, but since it's your daughter's wedding, may I just say that..." He paused to clear his throat. "Well, I might think again about that choice of caterer. Lots of caterers in town!"

"Oh?" I fixed my expression into a look of concern. "Have you heard something bad?"

"Let's just say they provided food for my daughter's wedding. She married earlier this year. And, well, as I said, lots of caterers in town. Now, about that fine cigar—"

"I must say, I am confused. I have always heard nothing but good things about that vendor and their food. Could you be specific? Because I am concerned." I gave him a small smile. "I suppose your daughter might have been a lot like mine. She has planned her wedding since she was five or six! And if the flowers or the food were to be a disaster...well, I don't think I could stand it."

He stared down at his loafers. Salvatore Ferragamo; I took note of the brand. That was a lot of cigar sales.

"Look," he said, "I have told Althea—the partner that I dealt with—that I wouldn't talk about it. I gave her my word. After she gave me a refund and assured me that the...problem has been fixed. So I am afraid I may have said too much already. I hope you understand. You just seem like a nice lady, and as a dad myself, I would hate to see your daughter disappointed when it comes to her big day." He moved a little closer and spoke very quietly. "So, for her sake, I urge you to rethink your plan."

"Hmm. But several people that I know are also getting married, and I'm sure that they'll *insist* on using them as well. They are like an institution here! They've been around so long." I gave him a hopeful smile. "If you could, perhaps, be just a *wee bit* more specific, you and I could save a lot of brides from a lot of tears."

What problem could there be that Althea had to fix?

"Well, the thing about it is, I may bring legal action. Althea Lindstrom can give me back my money, but she can't go back in time and give my daughter back her day. And I've been told by counsel not to say a word. But since I've opened my big mouth, you can warn your friends. Just don't say it came from me."

Ten minutes later, I walked out with something called a "Bolivar Beliscoso Fino," sealed in plastic and gift-wrapped. My new friend assured me it was earthy and full-bodied and that my "son-in-law" would love it.

Someone would love it, I was sure. I just had to determine who.

As he held the door open for me, I saw him turn the sign that said the store was closed. Then a cell rang in his pocket, and he took it out. "That's my lawyer now," he said. "So very pleased to meet you, and I hope you'll come again—now that you are welcoming a cigar man to your family." He gave me a smile.

I lingered at the clothing shop nearby, pretending to do a little window-shopping. How convenient would it be if I could "overhear" him talking to his lawyer when he came out of his store?

Which is how I ended up following him and the Dalmatian to the dog park down the street.

Gatsby let out a happy yip when he saw where we were heading, and I tried to quieten him. "Let's not be too obvious," I whispered, "but this worked out well for you. Lots of walks today!"

CHAPTER FOURTEEN

I stayed far back enough that Benson (I hoped!) wouldn't notice me. But I could hear him talking—angrily—on the phone.

Angry—that was good. I could hear angry from a distance.

"A full refund just won't cut it." The more furious he got, the more he picked up speed, which *wasn't* an advantage. I hadn't worn the right shoes to keep up with his pace, but I was determined.

"It was my daughter's only wedding!" he continued. "And what memories does she have? People *fleeing* the reception, knocking down the punch bowl in their rush to find the bathroom—or a tree to hide behind and throw their dinner up."

Now, I was just confused. That could *not* be Honey's food. What was he going on about?

I picked up my pace even more in an effort to keep up, and that was a thrill for Gatsby. I loved a nice, *slow* walk, but Gatsby not so much; he loved to run and zoom—which is why I took him to the dog park as often as I could.

"Picture the scene if you will!" My new cigar-aficionado buddy was still on a tear. "Everyone in the reception hall is white-faced or bent over double," he yelled into the phone. "All of them are sick." He paused to listen for a moment. "That amount is an insult to my daughter and her fiancé Glenn. And to me as well! Do you know how much I paid for that band from California? And instead of top-forty hits and jazz, what is the sound you hear? The sound of people retching! Instead of dancing to the beat, they're writhing to the pain. Someone has got to pay."

His energy got Gatsby all riled up, and he barked in agreement.

Which was a major uh-oh moment.

Benson whirled around and looked at me with suspicion. I could see his mind at work, wondering if he was being followed by a crazy woman. I had been super eager for the details about Honey and Althea and what had gone so wrong. And now here I was strolling close behind him in the dark. And on a sidewalk, too, where nearly all the stores were closed. He must surely have me pegged as the eavesdropper that I was.

"Just browsing!" I called brightly. "I always like to window shop, and this window caught my eye. Just the thing I need!" I turned to my right to see which window I was currently in front of. "Cecil Simmons," said the sign. "Criminal Defense. Major Felonies and White Collar Crime." *Okay, not so perfect.*

"In some trouble, are we?" Benson frowned. The Dalmatian cocked its head to study me, and I could see suspicion mounting in the eyes of the man who once had been so friendly.

"Oh, so nice to see you! But my house is two blocks that way." I pointed to my left. "And I need to get on home."

"Well, good luck with...all of that," said Benson, looking once again at the lawyer's sign. Then he resumed his walk and his conversation.

I thought to myself I should probably go home and leave bad enough alone. He could look back any second! Then again, I might miss hearing some good stuff. So I continued on.

Probably because of me, he kept his voice low at

first. Then the call once again got heated. "We can't get more than that for our pain and suffering?" he shouted to the lawyer. "And the honeymoon! They had to leave a day late. The groom's stomach was a mess, and there was no way he was getting on a plane—or more than ten feet from a bathroom."

Eliska from The Cake Shoppe stepped out of her door with a plate of homemade dog treats when she saw the Dalmatian.

And I knew I was in trouble.

As I knew he would, my enthusiastic dog strained against the leash. Gatsby was an ardent fan of those very treats.

One, unfortunately, cannot explain to a dog the fine art of subterfuge. But we needed to stay back. We were, after all, supposed to have veered off to the left, the direction of "my house."

Benson paused in his conversation long enough to signal with a nod that his dog could have a treat.

Eliska bent down with the plate. "Made from peanut butter and pumpkin just this morning. Only for the best dogs! And do I see a good dog? I believe I do!" she cooed. The Dalmatian sat at attention and gobbled not just one but two of the bone-shaped treats.

Benson finished up his phone call and turned to the

bakery owner. "Thank you, Eliska. That was kind. At least someone in this town knows how to mix ingredients in such a way that does not disturb the peace."

"Does not...disturb...the...*what?*" Eliska looked confused.

"Oh, just never mind. Having a bad day. But not Pippa here! Look what a happy girl. Peanut butter is her favorite."

It, unfortunately, was Gatsby's favorite too. He knew those two words well. Soon, he was flying down the street with me barely able to hold on to the leash and not trip over my feet.

"Gatsby!" Eliska was delighted. She bent to let him lick her face. "I thought of you this morning when I baked these treats. I was hoping you'd be by. And you are just in time! I was just closing up." She gave him one treat and then two. Then she looked on, pleased, as he devoured her creations and panted happily.

I breathed hard to catch my breath, and Benson raised an eyebrow.

"Lose your way?" he asked. The man was onto me.

"Well, you know how these dogs are. He loves his exercise. But now I *must* get home. Early day tomorrow, and Gatsby's a tired boy."

Benson simply nodded and turned toward the dog

park, which was all lit up, right across the street from Eliska's shop.

Gatsby yipped, excited, when he recognized the fountain with dog statues, where he loved to play.

Pippa ran to Gatsby, extending her front legs and lifting her rear into the air. In the doggy world, I knew that meant, "Come on, let's play!"

Gatsby replied with a happy bark, and soon a frowning cigar merchant and an embarrassed bookstore owner found themselves being pulled into the park.

I sat as far away as possible from Benson and tried not to meet his eye as our two canine companions blissfully ran and played.

After a long silence, he frowned doubtfully at me. "A tired boy, you say?"

"Well, he loves the park."

We continued after that to quietly watch our dogs.

"I don't know what you heard," he said after a while. "But I absolutely mean it. Not a word."

"I didn't hear a thing." I waved away his worry. "Oh, but what a shame. *Her wedding.*"

He shook his head, disgusted. "Ugliest seven words in the English language: Asian Fried Chicken with Honey-Ginger Sauce." He looked me in the eye. "Let that be a warning to all mothers of the bride. Just do not do it. *Please.*"

Thomas's special sauce. His beloved final product—the supposed crown to his legacy in the gourmet industry. That assault on unsuspecting stomachs, it would seem, had been the source of all the turmoil at Spoonful of Honey.

Time for another talk—and soon—with Althea.

CHAPTER FIFTEEN

he next day, the phones seemed sadly quiet as Althea arranged some cheese straws on a platter and slid them into the display underneath the counter. She handed one to me. "They shouldn't go to waste, and—as you can see—the phones aren't ringing off the hook."

"It will pick up with the season." Fourth of July, Father's Day, beach parties. Althea and her business should be just fine, I thought. As long as word didn't spread about the "special" sauce.

I took a bite and nodded. "A little kick. It's good."

A paperback lay face-down on the counter, and I could see a game of Candy Crush was paused and waiting on Althea's phone.

She saw where I was looking. "Slowest that we've ever been."

Because of the sauce fiasco? And how extensive was it? I needed her to talk—and I had a name. I could not break Benson's trust, but I could mention Martin, who had called the shop when I was there before. He had seemed to be as fired as Benson, judging from Althea's end of the conversation.

"It can't be all that bad," I said. "One of our customers brought up your name the other day. His name, I believe, was Martin."

Althea flinched and then locked eyes with me, instantly alert. "What did Martin tell you?"

"Oh, I just overheard a snippet of a conversation. I didn't catch a lot." Then I grabbed her hand when I saw her expression. She was close to tears, which was *so* not like Althea. "Althea, what's the matter? What is going on?"

"Honey-ginger sauce!" she said. "It might have ruined us, Rue. I told Honey, and *I told her* this would be major trouble, but would she listen? No!"

Bingo.

"I don't know what you mean," I said. Oh, of course I did; I was putting it together, some of it at least. But I needed details.

Althea reached below the counter and pulled out one of the familiar jars with the yellow label and the silhouettes of three cockatoos. "Honey's Uncle Thomas seemed to think this stuff right here was poised to be the product of the year. But, Rue, this stuff is...well, I would give you a taste, but this is beyond nasty. And it's more than just the taste; it rips your insides out. Like you either want to move into the bathroom and just live there for the day—or curl up in a ball and wish the world would stop. Honey tasted it, and she warned me not to. But I didn't listen." She screwed up her face. "Unbelievable."

It still did not make sense. Over its long history, Carroway Fine Honey had enjoyed top rankings—repeat business! Major industry awards. And it didn't get there by making sauces that were duds, unfit for consumption.

I took the jar from Althea and turned it over in my hand. "So, what is the deal?" I asked. "For the first time in their storied history, have they forgotten how to taste-test and do quality control?"

"Well, most people haven't, but Thomas doesn't think straight, and ever since the man got sick, there's been a loss of trust. He didn't trust the others at the business to have any kind of hand in the refining and perfecting."

"With the way his mind was going, they should have known that would be trouble. How was that allowed?"

"The decline was kind of sudden. And from what Honey told me, he didn't do a lot in the last month or so, just wrote ideas in a notebook and forgot that they were there. But then came the sauce! This sauce was his baby, the last great thing he'd do. Without anybody knowing, he went outside the company to have it made and bottled, made up the recipe himself."

"Oh no."

"His mother's recipe, he said. But he must have added something extra. Or put in twelve cups of *whatever* when it should have been just one. Who knows what's in that stuff." She sighed. "Well, so anyway, the bottles of the stuff came into the mansion, boxes and boxes of it. From some place overseas he had found to make it up and do the packaging. Honey very quietly stuck it in a closet. But first she tasted it—and *wow*. She shut the closet door on that stuff. And a while there, all was good. It was like the whole thing had just slipped his mind."

"Too bad that didn't last."

"It might have been okay. Except that one day, Uncle Thomas came into the shop to say hello to Honey. His doctor told him he should walk, and so one of the staff members would walk with him downtown, up and down the sidewalks. And one day he walked over to our shelf of sauces—and his wasn't there. Well, that wouldn't do. The look in the old man's eyes—Honey said it broke her heart. It was a source of tension between the two of them. She told him we preferred to concentrate on vinegars and jams, that we were mostly caterers. But he accused her, Rue, of not being loyal to the family name. How dare she refuse to promote his fine creation to the people in the town? Then when she suggested that perhaps the experts at the downtown office do some tweaking with the ingredients, it was like she'd slapped the man. The Carroway name, he said—and anything to do with honey—were her family legacy. How dare she refuse? Honey told me she could tell he was more hurt than angry, despite the fighting words. And Honey, she gave in. She insisted that we 'stock' it."

"Are you kidding me? No way!"

"Just for show, she said. Just for him to see when he stopped by the store." Althea ran her hand through her hair. "Can you see where this is going?"

Oh, yes. Yes, I could.

"We watched that stuff like a hawk, bound and determined not one of those bottles would ever leave the store. But then..." She looked down at the floor. "Why did he do it, Rue? While Thomas was a great *idea man*—in his time, at least—he never was the best with ingredients and such. That never was his thing, but until recently, he stayed in his lane and left that to the pros." She paused. "In fact, Honey told me once that most of the higher-ups think some of the sauces from his time had extra little twists that weren't his ideas at all. But who really knows?"

Clem knew, I decided. Thomas had spun some of his friend's ideas into major moneymakers.

I studied the small jar. How had that stuff made it into the chicken dish Honey and Althea had taken to the wedding?

"I loved Honey's heart," Althea told me, "but I told her that this horror in a bottle could turn into a nightmare for this business *I depend on, Rue.* I don't have family money like she always did to back me up if something happened to the business. And it turned out I was right. Trouble came and found us. Oh man, did it ever."

The chain of events, according to Althea, was set off by a CPA named Martin Anderson, who bought the sauce as gifts for his fiancée's mother and his most prestigious clients. Thus, with one swipe of his AmEx, he created havoc in both his love life and career.

"We were *vigilant* about not letting any of those things make it out the door in the hands of customers." Althea put her face in her hands. "But one day we had a temp, and somehow a bunch of the awful things got sold. People saw the label—Carroway Fine Honey—and they said to themselves, 'We'll eat gourmet tonight. No more boring pork chops! I'll try this on my meatballs! Honey-ginger noodles!' So many ways to turn a meal into an emergency."

"Oh." I felt for Althea.

"Three customers in all. We managed to convince them there had been a mix-up—a bottling mistake—and we plied them with free food. We *begged* them not to talk down about the business. And it was okay for a while. We had, after all, built a reputation here, and this is a fine town, full of understanding folks. Most of them were cool; some of them could even laugh about it—once their stomachs settled down." Then I saw a fury move behind her eyes. "But, Rue, here comes the worst part: Honey *still* insisted we keep those things on the shelf. Can you believe that, Rue? It was one thing not to want to hurt her uncle's feelings, but she also had an obligation to the business that we built."

According to Althea, people increasingly took notice of this new, intriguing product. They began to ask that honey-ginger dishes be served at their weddings and their parties. Honey got to work and created her own version of the sauce, which proved to be a hit. But then what Althea termed as "the dark day" occurred. One of the assistants grabbed the don't-touch bottles during the preparatory work for not one but *two* weddings.

Althea sank down on a stool and closed her eyes. "So the couples said their vows, and then the Olympics started with the writhing and the puking and the fleeing from the room. We agreed after that—that the stuff was gone, goodbye." A hard look formed in her eyes. "But we will have to see what it means for our reputation once things have settled down. A lot of people from the town were at those weddings, Rue. And they know exactly who catered the receptions."

My eyes went to the sauce jar in the trash. It was nestled against a book—on how to become a rising star in hospitality.

"Oh, yeah," said Althea when she saw where I was looking. "I was thinking this next year I'd go back to school. I've always had a dream of running a hotel—somewhere snowy in the mountains, a destination for those who love fine food. I would do the meals, and I'd pay other people for the kind of little details that would make the place stand out." She looked from the book to me. "Oh, Rue, I understand that must hurt your heart. A book! In the trash! But what good would it do me now? Sure, the business is still standing after all the "Sauce-Gate" stuff, but people like to talk. Will the money still be there for the next semester and the next? I'm no longer all that sure."

I wondered if her despondence was really all about her lost dream of a mountain paradise. Or did she regret her angry words at Honey during what turned out to be her cousin's final days on Earth?

Or did her regrets go deeper? One business partner furious, one business partner dead…

I felt immediately awful for that disloyal thought.

"Honey would have wanted you to go for it—your dream," I told Althea gently. "She would have helped you find a way. She would tell you still to try."

"Well, honestly, I blame her for the fact that book is in the trash. But I know you're right. The two of us were tight like sisters." She smiled at me sadly. "Some of the customers assumed that we were *really* sisters, although I'm not sure why. *Is your sister in? Your sister told me there would be vanilla scones on Tuesday.* And so sometimes we'd pretend with certain customers for fun. *Let me ask my sister. My sister made an apple trifle that you have to taste.*"

A chill ran down my spine as I thought about my visit with Clem and Helen.

"*How did Honey get home?*" I had asked Helen.

"*She called her sister.*"

CHAPTER SIXTEEN

*S*till reeling from the visit to Spoonful of Honey, I stopped by the Carroway headquarters and asked for Stephen Lowry. Luckily, I'd thrown a folder in my purse about Read with Somerset Harbor. It was an easy, popular promotion in which local merchants recommended favorite books. It got the merchants' names out before the public, and customers got a thrill from the little peeks into the minds of the people they did business with. Who knew their dry cleaner was a fan of medieval fantasy? And it had caused quite a stir when the octogenarian seamstress from Olga's Alterations chose to recommend *Still Spicy After Sixty.*

"Have you been talking to my wife?" Stephen smiled at me from the other side of his massive desk. "She is always telling me to turn the TV off and pick up a book. But, sure, I'll fill out your form and get it back to you. Perhaps a Sherlock Holmes..." He looked tired and distracted as he reached out his hand to the English pug who sat at his feet.

I gazed at him, concerned. "How are you doing, Stephen? What a rough week for us all."

"It's been tough, Rue. I won't lie. All of our hearts break for Thomas, and things here at the office? Well, they have been a little nuts. I have to say Bea Lindstrom let no time go by at all before she came marching in here with her uncle's files. He had been insistent he still 'play' at the job. But this death hit him hard. All his fight, I think, is gone, and he gave into Bea without much of a fuss." He gazed wearily out the window that looked out over the parking lot. His office was all windows and dark wood along with tasteful etchings of star products through the years framed in ornate gold.

"No kidding," I told Stephen. "Bea was on that real fast." *Take care of business, first; mourn your sister second?*

"Well, Honey was the one who would sometimes back him up when Bea insisted that he hang it up." Stephen let out a sigh. "And frankly all that stuff Bea brought us is just in disarray. His mind is going, Rue— more than we understood. Honey, we believe, had come to see that more and more. But Honey felt the work gave her uncle purpose, and she wanted that for him. But Bea not so much. Bea wanted to make sure all assets were protected. All business—that one, Bea."

"Well, it sounds like it was time."

Stephen scratched his head. "It's kind of like those puzzle books you sell in the store. Some of the things he wrote down in the notes must mean *something*, I suppose, but we can't work it out. He would write one word when he must have meant another. But what word would that be?"

Honey must have been engaged with the same kinds of puzzles. My mind traveled back to a certain drawing: the happy little trees that had seemed to worry her that last day at her shop.

"Luckily," said Stephen, "Archer, our accountant, keeps a close eye on the money. Any moves by Thomas would not have been a secret." He leaned back in his seat. "Honey reached out to Archer, worried, when she saw the kind of shape her uncle's mind was in. But mostly it was fine. He didn't seem to do a lot except to make some notes—utter nonsense, really—in his files." Stephen paused a moment and scratched behind his ear. "Although there were some mystery costs to a packager we didn't recognize, some fairly minor charges. A total mystery to us, but we have made some calls."

"Did you speak to Honey after she moved in with

Thomas?" I asked Stephen. "I kind of had the idea there was something on her mind." Someone had threatened Honey, I was almost sure, based on my last visit with her. She and Althea had their issues, but then so did she and Bea. I wondered if Stephen had a read on who had frightened Honey.

"She wasn't doing all that great if you want to know the truth," he said. "I got the sense that Thomas could take his anger out on her. When he would call the office, he seemed to have an issue with her...'genius-ology?' Ranted on and on about 'that newfangled nonsense my niece has taken up.'"

"Genius-ology? What in the world is that?"

He shrugged. "As I say, a lot of puzzles. And she and Bea were at odds about what to do with Thomas. Once they came in for a meeting. And in the parking lot, when I happened to look out, Bea was right in Honey's face. Going at her hard. I felt bad for Honey, almost stepped out to the car myself to intervene on her behalf. Bea can be a force."

I thanked him for his time and left the office with more questions than before.

I spent the rest of the day with a string of customers; everyone in Somerset Harbor seemed to have decided all at once it was a good day for a book. Intermittently, I tried to get in touch with Andy. He should know about the problems between Honey and Althea, but he did not pick up. I wondered if that meant things were moving on the case.

Finally, things slowed, and I settled in the Book Nook, our comfy reading corner, with a cup of tea as I watched Elizabeth organize some photos.

I told her about the reasons Althea might have been the one who had picked up Honey on the night she died —and then lied to police. "Which does not look good for her. On the other hand..." I filled her in about the way Bea had been so quick to put a stop to her uncle's dabbling with the fortunes of Carroway Fine Honey. Now that her adversary in that matter could no longer interfere. "I have so many questions." I took a soothing sip of the cinnamon-orange flavored tea.

"Well, tonight, come on over, and you can spend some time with Bea herself, and maybe that will help. She's bringing fabric samples for a chair and some 'accent pieces' that I am almost sure cost more than my car."

That might well be the case since Elizabeth drove her cars until they would no longer crank. Vintage was her style in every aspect of her life.

"You like puzzles, right?" I slipped off the too-tight flats I had bought on sale. While I dived into a mystery when I was feeling stressed, Elizabeth was different. She loved all kinds of puzzle books—which would make my heart rate increase if I couldn't get the answers right away. Patience was not one of my virtues.

"Hit me up," she said.

"Okay, you have a line of trees. They're different sizes, different shapes. And I'm talking trees with faces. These are *gleeful* faces, like someone in the forest has just told them a joke, a really, really good one."

Elizabeth paused in her work to visualize the picture I had just described.

"It's just some crazy picture that I saw at Honey's," I explained. "Is there some hidden meaning that you can figure out? What the heck does it mean?"

"Intriguing," said Elizabeth. "I'll give it some thought."

"Also, 'genius-ology.' That was some new thing Honey was involved in, according to her uncle—and it irritated Thomas."

Elizabeth leaned back and closed her eyes, which meant she was thinking hard. But she came up blank. "Come by at six," she said. "I have some tortellini soup with sausage, and I can heat that up for us."

Three hours later, Bea was setting a sculpture on one of Elizabeth's side tables. She looked at it and frowned before moving it to a long, tall table that sat behind the couch. "Much better," she pronounced.

Beasley peeped at us from underneath the couch. When I had stopped at a red light on the way over, a tell-tale mewing coming from the back seat let me know Elizabeth would have another guest. He had stowed away inside a box of socks and T-shirts, all with bookish themes. I had planned to drop them off for Somerset Harbor Cares, our local charity for families in need.

Bea wrote the price on a slip of paper and handed it, folded, to Elizabeth, as if that would make the numbers less intimidating.

Elizabeth opened up the missive and did a double-take.

"And that's without the eyes!" I joked. The abstract marble head had squarish shapes instead of features. Avant-garde, I guessed, but what did I know?

"It's hand-carved. Very fine," said Bea. "I believe it gives the room a subtle air of class. But of course, if it doesn't speak to you…"

Was there an insult in there somewhere?

"Is it a he or she?" I asked. I studied the piece of art with a genuine desire to understand. Because I didn't get it.

"It is gender non-specific." Bea took a breath as she moved a stack of books away from the statue and set it at an angle. "Live with it a while, see if it feels 'at home,'" she told Elizabeth. "Now, about that fabric for the chairs and ottomans."

We turned our attention to the couch, where squares in four different patterns were laid out in a row. I loved the rich gold with subtle bits of red and green. Then again, the deep blue put me in mind of the sea at twilight.

Then we turned our attention to the old brown chairs that might be getting a new look.

"I believe that any of the four selections will blend in very nicely with the colors that you have," said Bea. "All of the fabrics have an upscale richness, a soft feel against the skin; they have—"

Movement. They had movement—or one of them did at least. I turned my head in time to see the blue and plaid square scurrying across the couch before landing on the floor. A gray tail soon emerged from underneath it. Then the fabric settled into an "upscale" mewing lump.

"Beasley might be right." Elizabeth gazed down at the floor. "The plaid is rather nice."

I picked up the blue square and ran my hands across it. It was time to get on with my investigating. "I can't stop thinking about Honey." I turned to Bea, fixing my expression into a look of concern. "Now that some time has passed, Bea, have you thought of anything at all that might have frightened her?"

Why had Honey made that joke that I should send in the troops if she failed to show up at the party?

Bea reached into a satin box and set a glazed black panther on the mantle. Again, she wrote down a price and passed it silently to Elizabeth.

"Not so bad," said Elizabeth, her eyes moving from the paper to the accent piece.

"That would be the first of four installments."

Elizabeth put her hand to her mouth, then Bea turned to me. "Honey did seem troubled, but my sister's life was hectic. It would be difficult to think back now and pinpoint a single cause for her latest round of woe-is-me." A soft look came across her eyes, indicating the remark had been made with a fondness for her sister rather than derision. Honey's busy schedule had likely been a source of teasing between the Lindstrom women.

Bea angled the panther to the left. "I do know there seemed to be some complications of some sort at Spoonful of Honey. And then there were her different projects. You know how it was with Honey—always running here and there."

"Yeah. So many projects—like her genius-ology?" I

just threw it out there, because what the heck. It would be one puzzle solved.

Bea cocked her head, confused. "Her genealogy, you mean?"

"Oh! I didn't know that Honey had an interest in her family roots," said Elizabeth. "I could have helped with that. I have wonderful old photos of the Lindstroms and the Carroways, dating back, I think, to the eighteen hundreds."

"She did well on her own—although that stuff is fairly useless as far as I'm concerned." Bea frowned as she picked gray cat hair off the plaid swatch of fabric. "Why *look for* family members when life is hard enough with the ones you have?" She looked from me to Elizabeth. "Honey—if you can believe it—found another sister. That was not confirmed, but if you looked at Honey and then you looked at Lynn, well, then you had your answer loud and clear."

"Another sister?" breathed Elizabeth. "What a thing to find out."

Bea sniffed. "The last thing that I need is some new relation. Plus, I would have preferred to never know that ugly little fact about what my father had been up to on the side."

My mind went to the customer who thought he had seen Honey eating breakfast. *I had to turn around when I heard that girl's laugh,* he had told me in the store. Which was so very Honey.

I thought of the woman who had sat on Althea's row at Honey's funeral. From the profile, at least, she had looked so much like my friend that I had longed to touch her on the shoulder. To have her turn around, to be Honey in the flesh, still with us after all.

"And what did Thomas think?" I asked.

Bea looked down and hesitated. "Oh, I'm not really sure how much he understood. Failing mind, you know."

But I didn't think he liked it, based on what Stephen had said. A long-lost relation might well arouse suspicion in the aging patriarch of a family with a fortune. Especially a man who had grown distrustful and more isolated in his final years.

If it had been this "Lynn" who had driven Honey home on the night of her murder, had her presence in his home stirred up something dark in Thomas?

"We agreed not to share the news with anyone just yet. Just the Lindstroms knew, and I believe that Honey had told Paul." Bea unboxed a marble lamp and set it on a table. "As I mentioned earlier, it has not yet been confirmed."

When Beasley peeped out from behind the gender-non-specific face, I quickly moved to grab him. If something were to happen, Bea, I had no doubt, would be specific with the price—horrifyingly specific.

"I am still just reeling." I stroked Beasley's fur. "And I know you are as well. And how devastating for your uncle. From what Honey told me, the two of them were close."

"Perhaps a little *too* close? She was always his protector. Which I understand. I get it. She knew it was hard for him to give up a job he loved, a job he once excelled at. But it was dangerous—to my inheritance and hers and to a lot of livelihoods. And in the end, it was dangerous as well to our uncle's reputation."

Bea did have a point, and I felt Honey had been wrestling in her final days with that problematic truth.

Bea let out a sigh. "He has grown furious, I think, with his own mind and its inability to function. He just goes on and on about things that make no sense. Like some paper he's misplaced, some big idea he has for an advertisement. Big bees and tiny bees, he told us, in a long straight line." She raised her eyebrow at us. "Now, does that sound like an ad campaign? Or a children's storybook?" She shrugged and picked up a square of fabric to hold against a chair. "He said his mother always liked the ads where the bees had faces. Friendly, happy faces that invited you to taste the honey and enjoy."

Elizabeth tilted her head just a little; she was nursing an idea.

"I can't imagine how it must have been for my sister in the end." Bea's voice had turned soft. "Don't you wish that one of us could go back in time? And say to her, 'Honey, please. Just put down that mug.'" Then her cell phone buzzed. "Be right back," she said, stepping toward the kitchen.

"Honey bees," mouthed Elizabeth, her eyes big with understanding. "The honey-ginger sauce was in honor of his mother, who liked ads with honey bees." She kept her voice very quiet. "And honey bees in an addled mind can turn into *happy trees.* It rhymes! Happy trees with faces."

Hmm. One puzzle solved? Perhaps.

Then Bea came back, looking white. "Girls, I need to go." I heard tears in her voice, which was barely a whisper now. "They've just arrested Thomas—for the murder of my sister."

CHAPTER SEVENTEEN

"I think you've got it wrong." Oliver nestled at my feet as I sipped my zinfandel, seated across from Andy on my porch.

"No, Rue. He confessed. I know his mind is messed up—even more so with the stress. But he had a solid motive. He was in the house alone with her as far as we can tell when it all went down. There were traces of the poison in that mug—and just two sets of fingerprints: Thomas's and Honey's."

"That doesn't mean that someone else could not have been there too. And put poison in the mug before Thomas handed it to Honey."

"The man is just despondent," Andy said, and he looked despondent too. "He said it was a fury that just came over him—that everyone, it seemed, was all up in his business, telling him to stop the thing he was meant to do." He grew very quiet. "The courts will take it easy on him because it's not hard to see his mind just isn't right."

I let out a sigh and petted Oliver as he crawled into my lap. "There's so much you don't know. Thus the million voicemails that you have from me."

His eyes grew wide above his drink. "Okay, Rue, go on."

"Helen said 'her sister' was the one who came to pick Honey up. But Andy, now I know that could mean Althea—or the *other* sister."

"The *other* sister, Rue?"

I explained about the third Lindstrom sibling.

"Are you kidding me? That's huge."

"They kept it very quiet. Or it could have been Althea who picked Honey up and was at the house that night." I explained the reasons why Althea could have been referred to as a "sister." I told Andy why Althea would have been furious at Honey on the night of her death.

"I really think you're wrong," I said. "This cannot be right." Thomas was the uncle who had set up water slides at the mansion and weaved magical stories for Honey when she was a girl. As confused as his thoughts were, a confession, in my mind, didn't mean a lot. Or perhaps that was my heart looking to somehow prove it could not be him.

In the growing darkness, the tip of a Bolivar Beliscoso Fino glowed as Andy brought it to his lips. "I had a feeling you'd track down Benson Francis at his store," he said. "We will talk tomorrow to Althea, and I will meet with Bea, see what I can learn about this other sister, maybe track her down. And perhaps someone will slip. A few key details of the murder scene had been kept hush-hush. So if a suspect mentions, for example, the blanket that was placed over Honey's body, that would put them at the scene."

Something hit me then. "Who knows about the mug?"

"It is common knowledge that Honey died of poisoning. But few people know the source. Just you and us and the killer. And now the DA too, as well as the attorney for Thomas Carroway."

"And Bea." I set down my wine.

Don't you wish that one of us could go back in time? And say to her, "Honey, please. Just put down that mug."

I rushed to explain. But before I could finish, Andy had stood up and was reaching for his phone.

CHAPTER EIGHTEEN

*T*wo days later, I arranged a table of new releases I had pulled for a display. "Feel-Good Reads," read one sign. "Get Your Happy Endings Here!" trumpeted another. It was just what our town needed as talk slowly turned from murder to the rising temperatures and the condition of the waves.

Every murder has a villain, but at least in this case, no one truly meant for anyone to die. The poison, an insecticide, had indeed been pulled out (and just as quickly put away) by Thomas Carroway, who had instantly changed his mind and been appalled by his desire, however brief, to take his niece's life.

Bea had fueled his paranoia with a rant against her sister, designed to get her out of his home. That would pave the way, Bea thought, to finally get Thomas out of the family's business before he could do lasting harm. Later, Bea had sobbed to Andy and the chief that she never dreamed he would go so far as to wish harm on Honey.

But despite the fact that he had changed his mind—and that Bea would have stopped him from adding poison to the mug—the sad fact was that Honey still took a fatal sip on her final night. Andy had explained to me how it all went down.

It had indeed been Bea who picked Honey up that night. When Honey ran up to her room to take a shower, Bea had seized the chance to have her uncle's ear. As he fixed two toddies in the kitchen, she spoke of Honey's "snooping" in his work affairs. With the way that things were going, she insisted, soon the brand new sister would be in the house as well on a constant basis, hanging out with Honey. And someone else would have the chance to get a peek at whatever little project Thomas might be working on. (Of course, she didn't mention that the sister would have no claim to the Carroway estate, being only a half-sister with no ties to Honey's mom.)

Thomas grew incensed, and Bea was shocked when he pulled some insecticide from underneath the counter and held it above a mug. Almost immediately, when Thomas understood what he was about to do, he broke down in tears and put the stuff away. The old man was in despair over what his madness had almost led him to do.

Bea left the house that night feeling shaken but not really thinking her sister was in danger—until she heard the news.

"So, I still don't get it," I had said to Andy. "Who poisoned Honey in the end?"

The cops believed there must have been some bits of poison that made it into the mug before Thomas changed his mind. "Bea and Thomas at that point were both in a state and we think they didn't notice," explained Andy. A mistake, of course, that proved fatal in the end.

Despite the guilt she felt, Bea was not about to tell her story to police and incriminate herself. And she preferred for them not to know she was even in the house—until she let a certain piece of information slip.

Now, two members of the first family of condiments were in the local jail. Both of them were more grieved by their roles in Honey's death than about their incarceration. Blessedly, in the case of Thomas, his mind had slipped even further. On many days he was oblivious about the tragic death of his beloved niece and that final mug of toddy.

I fell asleep to tears both nights since the story had

come out, but I allowed myself the luxury of staying up to read some of my all-time favorite books. We, after all, must take our comfort where we can. And Althea had come by to introduce me to Honey's "other sister," which was a nice surprise. The familiar smile and laugh brought something back to me I was certain had been lost.

As I continued with the new display at the store, my thoughts were interrupted by a booming voice. "Point me to the travel section. Going on a trip!"

I turned around to see a beaming Clem, who was flanked by Helen and his oldest daughter, Laine.

"Where are you going, Clem?"

"Well, I don't know just yet. I thought some of your travel books would give me an idea."

Word had spread that Thomas had indeed set aside some money for his old baseball buddy—a little "thank you," as it were, for the "borrowed" recipes. And recently he had asked his lawyer to release the funds ASAP and not wait until his death. Thomas had reasoned, it was said, that the things a buck could buy—travel, for example—might require one's knees and hips to be in working order. And that was not a given as the years went by for men the age of Clem and Thomas.

With the bequest to Clem having been in place since Thomas was much younger with his faculties in place, there should be no problem, Andy felt, with the release of the funds.

"We are thrilled and touched," said Helen, "and my vote is for Paris. But, oh, does my heart break for Thomas Carroway."

"A good man," Clem agreed. "It was the sickness that took over when things happened as they did. The man's mind is going, but his heart is still intact. I have no doubt about it."

"Can't lose with John Grisham!" called a loud raspy voice that startled all of us. "New releases to the right!"

"Ah." A smile broke across Helen's face as she turned her head in the direction of the speaker. "I see you got a gift as well."

"None of the staff, it turns out, will be working at the mansion," I explained. "And that meant that *someone* needed a new home." I smiled at the parrot.

"Candles for half price!" announced the bird as a young man wandered past his cage.

The man let out a laugh. "I'm not the candle type, but I might check out these mugs."

"He'll be quoting Shakespeare soon," said Clem. "A literary parrot."

"And he might tell Rue's secrets too—if we get very lucky," said Helen with a wink.

I moved my fingers across my mouth as if to zip my

lips, and we all shared a laugh as Laine came back with a book on Italy. The scent of seasons changing wafted through the open window, and the smells of summer seemed to promise better days ahead.

# # #

Thank you for reading! Want to help out?

Reviews are a crucial for independent authors like me, so if you enjoyed my book, **please consider leaving a review today**.

Thank you!

Penny Brooke

ABOUT THE AUTHOR

Penny Brooke has been reading mysteries as long as she can remember. When not penning her own stories, she enjoys spending time at the beach, sailing, volunteering, crocheting, and cozying up with a good book. She lives with her husband and their spunky miniature schnauzer, Lexi, and two rescued felines, George and Weezy.

Made in the USA
Middletown, DE
31 January 2022